Taboo Erotica Stories

Taboo Sex stories include Anal Sex, BDSM, Bisexual, Milfs, Gangbang, Lesbian, Threesome, and Much More

Kevin Marino

© Copyright 2020 - All rights reserved.

The content contained within this book may not be reproduced, duplicated or transmitted without direct written permission from the author or the publisher.

Under no circumstances will any blame or legal responsibility be held against the publisher, or author, for any damages, reparation, or monetary loss due to the information contained within this book, either directly or indirectly.

Legal Notice:

This book is copyright protected. It is only for personal use. You cannot amend, distribute, sell, use, quote or paraphrase any part, or the content within this book, without the consent of the author or publisher.

Disclaimer Notice:

Please note the information contained within this document is for educational and entertainment purposes only. All effort has been executed to present accurate, up to date, reliable, complete information. No warranties of any kind are declared or implied. Readers acknowledge that the author is not engaged in the rendering of legal, financial, medical or professional advice. The content within this book has been derived from various sources. Please consult a licensed professional before attempting any techniques outlined in this book.

By reading this document, the reader agrees that under no circumstances is the author responsible for any losses, direct or indirect, that are incurred as a result of the use of the information contained within this document, including, but not limited to, errors, omissions, or inaccuracies.

Table of Contents

Carolina's Temptation

For Carolina nothing was as in the past; she was on edge not knowing how Noah would take her consensual adultery. Yet, she felt empowered and independent. She was already financially independent since she had a secured job as a Sales and Marketing Assistant in the reputed Advertising firm called Metric Theory. And now when she had the independence of engaging in a sexual relationship outside her marriage with her husband's consent, she felt sexually independent. Not too many women enjoy that exquisite luxury or unrestricted freedom. Carolina began the entire thing with the idea that she will just tease Noah and will give him a genuinely vibe of his fantasy. But she got so psychologically involved in it that she couldn't resist the forbidden temptation. First time alone with Noah after that night, she discovered that he was, in reality, a cuckold; she could see it composed all over his face. It was reiterated and confirmed when Noah was overly obsessed with her succulent udders which bore the teeth marks of Dominic. Not only did he kissed those marks, but also experienced an explosive orgasm while kissing those spots. When they had a brainstorming discussion about her experience and vibes on his birthday, Carolina was indeed eased to discover Noah upbeat and understood that he was experiencing every one of the feelings of a genuine loving cuckold. Carolina had a magnificent encounter and immensely satisfying experience. Thus, she finally realized that it would be hard for her to overlook it.

Carolina couldn't help comparing the two indispensable men in her life. On one side was her better half, Noah, whom she loved so much and who was so caring, loving and admiring towards that he would never confine her in any cage. And then again was this new Herculean hunk Dominic, who drew out the crude desire, the raw lust in her; the true feelings which she had perhaps buried in the deep corners of her brain. Carolina felt loved and cared with her better half; however, ached for the hard touch of a man, a man who could fuck her with bestial wrath and utilize her body for his pleasure.

As for Noah, he couldn't believe his luck how his deviant fantasies got fulfilled. Although he was in tremendous excitement to watch his own wife get impaled on a mammoth big fat cock, somewhere in the corners of his perverted mind he felt insecure. Jealousy conquered his earthly senses when he realized his own legally wedded wife got the stimulating pleasures of the highest heaven which he was unable to provide her. Insecurities vanquished his moral feelings when his twisted mind faced the brutal question of what if his wife left him for Dominic. The jealousy and insecurity were so overpowering for Noah that he practically had to leave the cuckolding session in between and retreat to the guest bedroom to spend the rest of the night. His thoughts raced from one point to another never allowing him to sleep and calm down his stimulating excitements. But, then again, a peculiar enthusiasm poked his twisted soul and affirmed that he was experiencing the most blissful stage of his life by being a fortunate cuckold, by allowing his wife to be in the arms of another man who could easily fuck her brains out.

Almost after two weeks, the matter popped up in their bedroom once again.

Carolina grabbed Noah's hairs and groaned softly as he licked her pussy, "Yesss... that's it, baby..."

Noah moved his tongue between the pussy lips and lapped enthusiastically, feeling her intensifying excitement. As a matter of fact, he also was electrically stirred beyond limits as they were in sixty-nine positions and Carolina was delicately licking and stroking his hard erection.

"Was he rough with you," Noah murmured in a dry voice, marginally lifting his head from her groin.

"Don't stop..." Carolina pushed back his head as she was lying underneath him.

"Yes... he was..." Carolina flicked her tongue over his hardened pole. "He took me extremely forcefully and I loved that," she asserted stirring him further.

Noah realized this isn't only some made up story from her this really happened directly in front of him. He saw her ecstatic hip movements on Dominic's mammoth fuck pole, heard her uproarious groans and cries while Dominic fucked her; moans that he as her husband won't be able to make her do. He began to eat her with extraordinary vigor showering his oral tributes on her rosebuds while Carolina stroked and licked his erection with most extreme consideration to drag out the ecstatic pleasure as much as possible. Noah caressed her bubble butts and drove his tongue further into her moistening pussy and requested her to take him into her mouth.

The entire scene flashed back in his mind, how till the last moment he was absolutely unsure whether Carolina would just tease Dominic or will really do it with him. He couldn't trust it when she undressed and played along. As Noah replayed the erotic, twisted scenes in his deviant mind, he realized he couldn't keep going longer and thrust forward his pin dick into her mouth. Carolina too sensed her husband's urgency and quit teasing him and slurped in an enormous piece of the erection inside her hot mouth. Almost immediately he began to cum.

In the wake of having his pleasure, Noah earnestly concentrated on pleasuring his wife as she held her head with both hands and guided him. Carolina shut her eyes and relished in the euphoric excitement, yearning for the strong hands of Dominic on her body, his mouth on her succulent bosoms, brutally mauling, pinching and kneading her assets. She grabbed one hand of Noah and placed it over her boobs and groaned.

" Harder..." Carolina moaned, "take me...ugggg..." She kicked her crotch and shuddered into a hard climax.

"You know Dominic called today. We were online for a longer time." Carolina stated after they were done pleasuring each other orally and lay panting.

"What does he want now?" Noah was extra attentive.

"Well, you know. He's in Seattle handling a lucrative deal. He just called to check about the advertisement paperwork," Carolina sighed. "But, yes. He sounded too excited and asked me to continue from where we left," she put her head on his chest.

" What did you say?" Noah's heart pounded a thousand times faster.

" Of course, I won't," she replied instantaneously,

"however, I hope you realize I feel extremely terrible, I have led him into this."

Carolina hugged Noah tightly and continued, "He felt that I was in a terrible marriage with you." She sighed and continued again, "That's why it all occurred and he was insisting that we should meet. He was not ready to understand why I was saying no... so I told him the truth."

" What!!" Noah was shocked, "You let him know everything?"

"Yes obviously, I needed to make him understand that all was well, and will be well among us. That I am content with my husband... He understood at last and was chuckling at himself and his sheer luck to be tricked so easily."

"Oh!" Noah breathed.

"So what do you say, should we meet him?" Carolina sounded serious.

Noah felt a thousand bass drums pounding in his heart as he understood that his wife was requesting to be with another man. He cuddled nearer to her and kissed her delicately on her luscious lips.

"I don't have the faintest idea. What do you think?" His voice was more like a pleading than an inquiry.

"I never imagined that I could ever do it. But it happened... In addition, I believed that you would never let it happen in reality in spite of the fact that you were constantly amped up for it... I thought you would always let it remain as a twisted and wild fantasy of yours. Be that as it may, you did... and also, you are quite cool about it," Carolina talked slowly but intently, stroking his hairs. "Now, Dominic is insisting for it again... He says for the last time."

Noah was trembling in excitement as he heard her out, "Would you like to do it?" It seemed Noah was almost choking with fervor.

"Well, I think one final time won't hurt, will it? Obviously, if you approve of it," she murmured with equal excitement. Noah was no deaf and dumb to his wife's emotions and he too sensed it.

He felt an ache of envy; meeting the man who had fucked his wife's brains out, was never his wildest dream. But the idea that she needed another man to pleasure and please her stimulated his excitements. The fact that his wife had fallen for a far more potent man than him stirred him beyond limits and soon his floppy pin dick twitched with earnestness. The thrills from the fact that his better half was ecstatically pleased by a man were all that he thought. In his deviant fantasies, the other man never had a face or a feeling like Dominic; it was just sex, wild sex. However, at this point, Dominic was a real man about whom his wife was talking. Everything that happened or would happen would be without a doubt and she loved it and would love it more.

Whenever Noah was sleeping with his wife the 'other man' had been just between them to stir up their passionate stimulations; not physically present, but in his mind and in their role-play. It drove him insane and he essentially couldn't get Carolina's animated statement out of his mind, "He has left his mark on me." This was his most earnestly desired twisted fantasies; his educated modern yet traditional conservative wife with high moral values corrupted and taken by a potent man right in front of him while he watched. Although he couldn't continue the last time and left in the middle, he was optimistic to crack the nut this time. He couldn't forget the desire, the cravings, the wild lust all over when she melted like wax in Dominic's embrace. He kissed her all over her body emptying his passion. Noah was subconsciously being protective towards Carolina as though she was some valuable possession, which was on the verge of being snatched away by a foreign invader.

Although Carolina promised Noah that what happened between her and Dominic and was just a one-time affair and would never consider it again, her determination debilitated when Dominic called her. Her perverted mind reminded her how intensely erotic the experience was nevertheless she figured out how to slow him down. In any case, just two weeks passed and she was thinking about giving the desire a chance to manage her rather than her mind, 'one final time and after that never again, she will be a good wife again.'

So it was fixed and Saturday night they were meeting Dominic at his home for supper. Dominic had already from Seattle and was dying to grab Carolina in his arms. Carolina too was keen to meet him almost after three weeks and fly the highest heavens of pleasure. Carolina came out of the shower wrapped in a towel, water dribbling from her wet hairs. She grinned and sat before the dresser drying her long wet hairs. Regardless of how frequently Noah had seen her like this, still it never failed to stimulate his arousal. She unknotted the towel and grabbed yellow panties from the cabinet. Noah keenly watched her slipping into the tiny piece of silken fabric over her buxom buttocks. The panties looked much smaller compared to her tempting curves and seductive lush framework, only the two triangles in the front and back. The front triangle was hardly able to conceal the prized rosebuds; so puffy and swollen yearning to be tribute with potent juices. Noah was hypnotized watching the swollen mound desperately trying to hide behind the tight fitting.

"Enjoying what you're seeing?" Carolina blushed as she asserted, "go out and wait for me," she affectionately rebuked him and he reluctantly strolled towards the living room.

Noah settled down on a couch, finding his mom, dad, and his distant relative Jordan enjoying the live auditions of America Got Talent. Noah's mom Theodora was 46 years old, still very youthful and jubilant in her spirits. Noah's father Trevor was 66 years old, a struggling man with his health. Jordan Murugan was 55 years of age and a distant brother of Trevor and very close family companion. Almost 15 years back when Trevor was struggling to settle down in the USA, Jordan helped Trevor and Theodora with all his resources.

"Amazing!! What a singer," all of a sudden Theodora screamed in excitement at the TV. Noah was snapped out of his trance and hastily gazed at the TV.

"Where were you lost son," she asked, "you never miss live auditions of AGT."

"I was just thinking about a designing plan and I can always watch the repeat telecasts," Noah pointed out at the repeat telecast of the show flashing in the corner of the screen.

"Since when did you begin contemplating working at

home," his dad Trevor stared at him in an amusing way.

All of them laughed out loud at Trevor's hilarious comments including Carolina who just walked into the living room and heard what her dad-in-law said. Noah realized it was all in amiableness and he too giggled at his dad's sense of humor. He glanced at his better half and discovered her as the same loving and caring wife, responsible and kind-hearted daughter-in-law taking care of the family whenever the in-laws would arrive. However, his mind was troubled to envision that she was the same woman that night that fulfilled his deviant fantasies and the one who was prepared to go out with him again to meet her stud lover.

"Wow Carolina!! You look extraordinary, so sexy," Theodora yelled enthusiastically as Carolina ventured out of the bedroom wearing her new sleeveless and backless maxi, a blue one this time. The backless design was enough to exhibit her lush back and it promptly showed she wasn't wearing any bra. Carolina grinned at her youthful mom-in-law's prizing compliment, "Thanks, mom. And you better be in bed early because tomorrow morning you three need to attend the charity function," she educated her while Theodora made a terrible face. "That's my Carolina. Always keeping the family in line." Acknowledged Jordan. Trevor, Theodora, and Jordan were in the management body of a charitable trust taking care of privileged children and helping them in their higher studies and healthcare.

Theodora although in her mid-forties, never showed any mark of aging neither in her face nor in her spirit. In fact, with every passing year, her glamour and elegance manifested God made beauty. Unlike Carolina, she was a more or less authoritarian in Noah ' s family being his mother. Besides, she maintained a strict glamorous lifestyle and as a hardcore feminist always believed in female independence. Her buxom bottom and perky chest mounds were enough to turn around any man's head and corrupt his spirit even in her mid-forties.

Theodora realized her son Noah and daughter-in-law Carolina won't be back till morning as her daughter-in-law had already disclosed to her that if Noah got drunk excessively, she won't drive back home late in the night. Noah was an occasional drinker only for parties and gatherings. Carolina never disclosed to her mom-in-law what party they were going to attend though. Theodora grinned as she realized that the house would be hers for tonight; her husband had heart problems and would soon retire to his bedroom as he had already taken his dinner and pills; and the maidservant would leave around 8:00 PM. She planned to sleep with her sweetheart Jordan in his room for tonight. Yes, that was absolutely true. Theodora and Jordan had been physical since the time they were struggling to settle down in the USA. "Nothing comes free in this world," was Jordan's assertion and Theodora cordially accepted his proposal enabling her husband to get a lucrative job and settle down in the USA. However, unlike Carolina who was mindful about Noah's feelings, Theodora was cheating on Trevor with Jordan for almost over twenty years now. In fact, Theodora was somewhat bewildered when it came to her hearty relationship with Trevor and physical relationship with Jordan. As days passed, she was so confused with her relationship status that she decided to end her relationship with Trevor. But Trevor had a serious accident then and Noah was too young as a five-year-old kid to take care of his dad and family. So, plans changed and since then she had been physical with Jordan. Jordan never married because he was her de facto husband.

Noah drove the Jaguar and every now and again glanced at his ravishing and gorgeous wife sitting beside him on the front seat. Carolina drove her long hairs back and kept on looking forward into the passing city lights and night sight. Noah was battling the urge to turn around his car, to drive it back and protect his most prized possession while Carolina was torn apart into pieces between the feelings of wild lust for Dominic and passionate love for Noah. She was apparently unable to stare at her husband and even utter a single word. The cold breeze from the car window caused goosebumps to course through her glowing skin and made chills flow down her spine. They reached, according to plan at Dominic's residence at around 7.30 PM.

"Hello!" Dominic welcomed them at the door. He was grinning and let out his hand forward to Noah. Noah warmly greeted Dominic murmuring something of a welcome as he escorted them inside. But that chuckle, that grin had a faint touch of humiliation and Noah' s heart skipped a beat when he realized Dominic's tone.

They ventured into an enormous and luxurious living and drawing room area and settled themselves on the couch. Noah fidgeted anxiously not understanding what to state under the uncomfortable circumstance; he felt too intimidated to speak. He glanced at his wife from the corner of his eyes for help yet discovered none; she too was a little uncomfortable as a result of her own conflicts and blushed taking an inquiring look at the neatly decorated hall.

"Wow man!! You are simply great," all of a sudden Dominic addressed Noah, "you are one hell of a daredevil to dare something like this," he concluded excitedly and Noah just returned the favor as he smiled sheepishly.

"That is a strikingly bold and daring step for both of you to transform your fantasies into realities," Dominic continued, "You tricked me well that night," he roared with laughter. The grin and giggling seemed, by all accounts, to be cordial and Noah felt somewhat relaxed as he couldn't discover those arrogant looks which stated 'I am the man fucking your wife, mate.'

"It was not our aim to trick you," Carolina clarified, "it was just instinctive," she talked reluctantly. As time progressed, Noah felt as if being left out as Carolina and Dominic continued to flirt and talk with each other.

Arriving at the room where Theodora was waiting for her lover, Theodora blushed to see Jordan and stating, "How's my slut doing for the night?"

Theodora was absolutely stupefied at the lecherous comment of Jordan especially when her husband Trevor had just closed his eyes. Theodora shushed and seductively twisted herself on the bed provoking Jordan's arousal. Trevor's once upon a time faithful wife Theodora gestured Jordan to have his seat beside her on the bed. The potent stud was in his sleeveless, short exhibiting his enormous swelling muscles.

Theodora felt her heart beating like drums, her entire

body shuddering with excitement when she recollected how this hunk man looked in the buff. Her significant other had a pleasant looking body for his age, however he was no muscle god like Jordan. As time passed, Theodora allowed her wild lust to corrupt her spirit and licked her lips seductively to tempt Jordan more. Her mind was flooded with sinful thoughts of how she was going to fly the highest peaks of lust with her lover.

Her line of reasoning was cut when Jordan unexpectedly jumped on her and kissed her feverishly on the fleshy lips. Her first response was an absolute shock, but afterward, she melted like wax in the amorous warm embrace of her lover, Jordan. He seemed to devour her luscious lips with his huge thick lips. His course tongue invaded her juicy mouth to meet with her soft tongue and swap saliva.

Dominic played a decent host and served drinks while Carolina took just sodas; Noah was upbeat as he required a solid drink to calm down his nerves. They had food and drinks and snacks which Dominic had ordered from a nearby restaurant and kept on talking while Noah was quite reserved. Dominic figured out how to bring the point back over and over on the night he spent with Carolina. He showered her with praises and recommendations like how strong she was, how independent and matured, she was and how her qualities perfectly blend in with her seduction. Carolina seemed to enjoy the flirts and compliments and started to open up more as time progressed. She even told him that he was his secret crush in the office, which made Dominic chuckle wickedly.

"It would be truly exciting for you," all of a sudden he addressed Noah, "So, how you feel about being a cuckold for real?"

Noah was gravely embarrassed by such an immediate inquiry and was not prepared for it. He looked at Carolina who was reddening too. He didn't have the faintest idea what to state as his face turned red with humiliation.

"In any case, I should state it's extremely unfair for me," Noah finally talked, "While you two were enjoying yourselves I was completely in the dark and just thinking about the stud that was able to seduce my better half." He talked in such a voice as though he was the victim.

"Are you complaining?" Carolina inquired.

"How could I complain!" he grinned, "It was a night I would always remember," he moved adjacent to Carolina.

"Oh! My man! I believe you walked away from the scene," Dominic giggled in a derogatory tone and continued, "Besides, you can always watch us. Can't he, dear?" He turned his face toward Carolina.

"I must confess I have never seen such an excellent, adventurous and brave lady," Dominic held Carolina's hand as he moved beside her. Noah felt hurt as he was half expecting that Carolina might push his hands away yet she didn't do anything. "What is he thinking? This is the reason they are here... she is here to fuck him." Noah wondered in his own mind as he discovered Carolina gleaming in fervor and extremely glamorous. "But every last bit of her glamour is going to be ravished by this man." Noah breathed hard as jealousy conquered his senses. All he could do was to take a big gulp of his drink.

Jordan was a true lion as always ravishing Theodora's lush framework. His hands were all over her body, squeezing her succulent bosoms with full force that drove her to the point of excruciating agony, pressing and slapping on her juicy pussy. But then again, Theodora lived the blend of pain and pleasure. He always yearned for her man to be rough and hard with her.

The pressure, the powerful sexual ministrations and the tempting imagination of his naked body on her were a lot for her. In two minutes Theodora was shivering in lecherous wants. She found herself topless with brawny lover sucking voraciously at her perky nipples, kneading them, chewing them, licking them while his hands were mauling her enormous bosoms.

Theodora had never given anybody a chance to ravage her like that. Her husband Trevor was so gentle on her unlike this bull ravishing her. Pushing at her nightgown, Jordan obliged the caring mother and cheating wife to take it off and soon the panties followed.

There she was, a married traditional Conservative mother, absolutely stripped on the bed with a brawny stud, being sexually utilized by a man who wasn't even her husband. Jordan was a specialist in dealing with married women and especially MILFs who had decent loving husbands like Trevor. He always knew how to liberate the whore inside them; the true woman that their decent, loving husbands did not know even existed. That was the charisma by which he had been penetrating Theodora behind her husband's back.

Taking his left hand, Jordan grabbed Theodora's moistening pussy and started to play with it and press on it. A deep lustful groan escaped Theodora's mouth. These were stimulating sensations that she had always experienced whenever she was with Jordan. Without notice, Theodora felt one finger penetrating into her sacred chamber as one of her perky nipples was all the while being chomped, kneaded and sucked voraciously by Jordan.

She bounced a little pleasurable excitement on the bed and snaked her hands on his huge muscular forearm desperately attempting to push it away. Rather, Jordan shoved his finger further into the cheating wife's pussy. Theodora felt her juices streaming and she was not able to resist any further the brutal ministrations of her lover. She let him keep on fingering her.

Carolina was feeling anxious as Dominic pulled her closer and she looked towards Noah. She realized this was going to give him heartache; however, he needed to experience this agonizing suffering to accomplish what he was longing for. The real happiness of being a cuckold is in the agony to see your wife in passionate and desperate lust for another man and realizing that she appreciates him utilizing her for his masculine endeavors. Carolina relaxed in Dominic's arms.

There was an uncomfortable and unusual silence in the room with the exception of the clamor of the AC system. Dominic caressed her delicate body in his arms passionately moving his palm over her hairs, cheeks, and neck. Noah squirmed with his glass and made an effort not to look at them. He felt furious with Dominic for touching her so affectionately and sensually and with Carolina for succumbing to his smooth traps. "Why don't you just fuck my wife and get done with it?" his perverted mind screamed helplessly, "Just take out your enormous big fat cock and shove it inside her pussy." Furthermore, he was extremely infuriated when Dominic turned her head and put his mouth over her trembling juicy lips.

Noah watched in anguish as Dominic kissed her luscious lips and Carolina's eyelids gradually shut and mouth opened to kiss him back. Noah felt impossible to breathe as he watched their tongues meet and exchanged saliva. He understood with a sickening dread that he had no power over this reality. Dominic wasn't simply going to put his mammoth cock inside her; he would likewise explore his ravishing wife's entire body with sheer amorous intent, the manner in which he was to be permitted to do. He wasn't simply going to fuck her; rather he was going to make her fall for him, crave for him and finally conquer her lively spirit. Dominic's one hand was now on Carolina's blouse and he was mauling her firm and ample tits with full force. He couldn't bear it any longer and nearly jumped up from his seat. His abrupt advancement diverted Carolina and she opened her eyes only to find him standing right in front of her and gazing intently.

"Are you OK, hon?" Carolina was frightened.

Noah couldn't answer and he just poured himself another drink and stared away from them feeling helpless and humiliated. Carolina understood that he was in excruciating agony; she squirmed out of Dominic's hold and rushed to Noah and embraced him firmly showering kisses all over his face.

"I love you, sweetie," Carolina cooed a few times and kept on kissing Noah.

Dominic was outrageous as his fuck toy slipped out of his hands. He gritted his teeth, "You filthy perverted asshole... why he has to interfere?" He was furious, unable to calm down his temper at this undesirable intrusion and wanted to kick his ass out of the room.

Noah was amazed and furthermore extremely jovial when he found out that Carolina was so worried about him. He felt most elated to realize that Dominic was just her fuck toy and had no place in Carolina's heart; he was the sole conqueror of her heart no matter the circumstances. In any case, his joy was brief as she held his throbbing cock and chuckled, "You... you... you scared the shit out of me... you naughty boy."

"Sweetie, I know it's hard for you to watch," Carolina stroked his hairs and talked intently, "Why don't you just chill in the extra room?" Noah was disheartened; his heart skipped a beat at the heartbreaking proposal.

" I will let you know everything in the morning," Carolina murmured deviously and then winked.

" Morning!! She already made plans to spend the whole night with him," Noah didn't have a clue what to state. Dominic, who was listening to everything patiently and impatiently, ventured closer as he didn't want to relinquish the brilliant chance. He embraced Carolina from behind jabbing his hardened erection on her ass.

"Why are you getting so restless?" Carolina snickered while Dominic pulled her away from Noah. He turned her around and gripped her in his masculine arms like a hawk gripping its prey. Noah watched her as she squirmed and giggled in his arms.

Back at Noah's place, Noah's mother Theodora was enjoying her ecstatic pleasure rides with her lover Jordan. Removing his pajamas, Jordan remained in his messy shirt while being totally stripped starting from the waist. Before he came to grab her, Jordan removed his boxers. This way it is quicker. Jordan sensed that the married cheating mother's cunt was well lubed from her own juices so he lifted her up in his masculine arms and let her down on his huge erect pole. When the precum covered cock head of the potent stud touched Theodora's cunt lips, a jolt of electricity coupled with a chilling flow shot through her entire body from her toes to her head.

Moaning a little louder as she was brought down on Jordan's huge fuck pole, Theodora felt her cunt being dilated. The first time she experienced such a wild feeling was when she brought forth her child, Noah. She had never experienced this feeling with her better half Trevor. Gradually, the conservative mother sunk on the big hardened erection until she was completely impaled on the masculine stud's monster. Theodora clutched the brawny broad shoulders of Jordan impaling her on his hardened manhood. She saw her wedding ring still on her hand as the symbol of her faithfulness, trust, and commitment to her loving and caring husband Trevor. Be that as it may, right now, she wasn't thinking straight, all her psychological power was concentrated in her cunt on the mammoth pussy breaker conquering her worldly senses. As Theodora raised and lowered her on the potent shaft, her succulent bosoms jiggled and loud sultry groans escaped from her throat as if she were being exorcised.

Theodora shut her eyes as the delightful ecstasy of pain and pleasure in her overstretched cunt overwhelmed her. "Is this how a woman should feel when she is filled to the brim with a masculine hunk's potent shaft?" Theodora wondered in her own euphoric delight. "Why do I miss all these stimulating pleasures with Trevor and only experience them with Jordan?" Theodora's amorous mind was crowded with all sorts of illicit questions. She was unable to make decisions; but, she knew a certain thing: The lustful delights she was experiencing, was from another man, Jordan, her ardent lover of twenty years who made her sit on a cloud high above, every time and anytime.

Dominic was too desperate for Carolina to delay the proceedings any further or to allow the married couple to reconsider their proposition. He immediately placed his mouth over her juicy lips and began to pull her maxi. Carolina wriggled feeling shy before her husband, yet Dominic figured out how to uncover her sexy thighs.

Noah watched the gradual and inevitable surrender of his better half into this Sturdy Hercules's muscular arms and the torment gradually transformed into a shivering sensation. He truly wanted his wife to make the most out of her ecstatic time with her lover and was no longer agitated as before. Dominic raised her maxi further and exposed the yellow panties, the tiny silken fabric scarcely covering her swollen sacred hole. His firm hands spread her smooth thighs further apart and squeezed the velvety pussy mounds causing Carolina to moan.

"Isn't she hot... would you please take her panties out for me," Dominic requested Noah with a sheer urge to take control of the proceedings. But his voice had more of a commanding tone than that of a request.

Undressing his wife for a sturdy man to fuck, was so humiliating for Noah; but, the idea itself sent chills of lewd sensation through his spine twitching his pin dick and making it leak with excitement. He saw his wife at him eagerly. He stood uncertain for an entire minute and then gradually proceeded to follow the orders of the man of the hour.

"Hold the maxi and don't give it a chance to fall back," Dominic asked Carolina who quietly agreed.

Noah stooped before his wife and unknotted the holding of the fine fabric. He stripped it off, revealing a well-moistened vagina. Jets of thin pleasure juices had flowed down her inner thighs as a proof of her own sensual stimulations. Noah was close that he could inhale the aroma of her excitement and he continued kneeling before her almost hypnotized by the excellence of the freshly shaven pussy.

"Much appreciated, cuck," Dominic asserted, "Now you can rest here while I take your wife to my bedroom. Obviously, it's better if you leave us alone and allow us to make the most out of it just like the other night... she would not enjoy your presence."

Noah wanted to watch Dominic fuck his wife this time; he was desperate to watch his mammoth big fat cock sliding all through his wife's married conservative pussy; he was dying to devour the sight of the nigger stud cracking the nuts in his wife's sacred spot. But he couldn't speak a word as Dominic gradually escorted her inside the room. Noah felt so alone, so abandoned as the door was slammed in his face.

Carolina relaxed once she was alone with her lover, Dominic, in his bedroom because in front of her husband she felt inhibited. Dominic pulled her closer to the bed and she traced the layout of his hardened erection through his sweatpants. She was eagerly waiting for this moment for the last couple of weeks; she eagerly pulled his sweat pants down and impatiently dragged down his boxers. She breathed heavily as soon as the big fat fuck pole waiting for its conservative pit throbbed in front of her face. Her eyes were about to blast out in sensual wonderment. Seeing his gigantic fat torpedo dancing in front of her, Carolina felt her pussy on fire. She took his mammoth fat cock in her warm mouth and sucked it for a few moments. The musky aroma of the potent shaft was enough to make her juices leak.

Dominic pushed her on the bed and moved over her, squeezing and mauling her succulent bosoms firmly. Carolina breathed out heavily, gasping for air at his hard touch and promptly the desire took over as she saw the masculine urges in his eyes. Chills gushed down her spine making her shudder like a leaf in a whirlwind. She felt the difference between raw, passionate lust of the Sturdy Hercules using her as a sex toy and the delicate lovemaking of her husband. Her mind was corrupted and crowded with corrupted thoughts as Dominic took control of her body. "My husband is in the other room. Make me scream your name out for him," Carolina chuckled deviously. Without further adieu, he raised her legs high and wide and thrust himself right in her flooding married pussy.

"Ahhh...Good God!" she tossed her head back in the wild ecstasy.

He began to pound her pussy hard. Carolina lay with her legs wrapped over his waist getting a charge out of each thrust. Dominic was in no rush and he fucked her harder and fucked her long. Carolina appreciated surrendering herself completely to his animalistic thrusts and came twice in quick successions which she didn't recall doing in a long prolonged stretch of time.

Noah was gazing blankly at the closed door of the room. He was shaking with obscure feelings, something which he had never experienced before as he heard the hard slamming of Dominic's erection into his wife's womanhood. His pin dick oozed juices and was agonizingly hard for a long time and he adjusted it before settling down on the couch again. He made himself another drink and took the glass to his parched lips with shaking hands. Sitting alone allowed him a chance to contemplate what he had done. He had carried his wife to her lover so that they can enjoy mind-blowing fucking. He had never observed his wife so excited and he felt jovial realizing that the Sturdy Hercules was fucking her brains out; her gorgeous lush body would be violated by a potent stud. Noah was on a high, a sexual high and he didn't want to jerk off as he wouldn't like to descend from that high. He realized this won't be the last time; there would be many more occasions like this. The sound of the bed rocking heavily sent chills gushing down his spine as the muscular virile stud performed his lustful duties.

Noah heard his wife Carolina screaming. And yes, Carolina was screaming as her legs were up high up in the air and the big fat cock pistoning all through her married pussy. She begged the Sturdy Hercules to fuck her hard, to stiff her with his big fat cock. She told him she worshipped him. She loved him more than her husband of 3 years when it came down to raw passion. Dominic on the other hand, made Carolina scream out his name and asserted to whom those married holes belonged. A great many orgasms shook her body as Dominic utilized her juicy bosoms and her flooding cunt for his pleasure. Their lips intertwined frequently as though they were a married couple performing their duty in their bed, just the cuckold husband was supplanted by a more potent male.

The fucking lasted several hours this time. The sheets reeked of cum and vaginal liquids as Dominic exhausted his overwhelming saggy balls inside the conservative wife's womb multiple times.

After the exceptional sex, they lay depleted in one another's arms. Carolina felt remorseful as she realized that she was doing this not for her better half's fantasy, but rather for her very own sexual satisfaction. She was frightened as she nestled with Dominic, she would not like to build up any affections for him apart from the raw animalistic sex. However, she couldn't resist her feelings and exquisitely relished being enveloped in his masculine arms. Carolina kissed Dominic on his smooth chest feeling the afterglow of sex and realized he would be hard soon. He prodded her to keep kissing him and pushed her head lower on his waist. Carolina recognized what he wanted.

Carolina slipped lower down all the way kissing and licking his body and stroking the flaccid pole. With her lustful eyes, she gazed him before taking him in her mouth.

"Ahhh...," Dominic groaned as the hot mouth engulfed his cock head. He felt control over this delightful lady who was extending her pretty lipstick decorated lips around his big fat cock. He set a hand on the back of her head and slipped his cock deeper in her mouth. The cock immediately extended to its most extreme and expanded her mouth. Carolina realized that what she was doing was way past the honorable obligation of an adoring wife; however, felt an unreasonable joy and a perverse pleasure, forgetting about every thought as she devoured and slurped on to the thick long fuck pole.

In her bedroom, Theodora felt the electrifying delight, she was given by Jordan's 8 inch fuck pole. Even if she added up all the love nights with her husband in twenty-seven years of her marriage, her husband Trevor was no match for this potent hunk who always drove her insane and gave her wings to fly the ecstatic pleasures of the highest heavens.

Jordan, all of a sudden, grabbed Theodora by her waist and she watched his muscles flexing as he moved her faster up and down on his throbbing erection. If anybody had ventured into the room discreetly, they would definitely consider Theodora to be a whore pleasuring the potent stud in the bedroom. But, Theodora didn't care for the world then. Her world was Jordan, shoving his potent shaft in her married pussy vigorously and using her as a fuck toy. Her lustful moans became more intense and Theodora muffled herself with her mouth not to awaken her cuck husband Trevor sleeping in the other room, as Jordan's gigantic erection filled her totally.

"I'm going to fuck your daughter-in-law slut? I'm going to make her my whore too?" Jordan breathed in Theodora's ears, sending chills of ecstasy down her spine.

"Please don't do that," Theodora's voice was husky. "She is my son's wife."

"She is a slut waiting to be freed just like you!" Jordan groaned.

To add to all this, Jordan started biting feverishly at the conservative mother's huge milk buckets. He was completely consumed by his overpowering lust for this fuck toy. What's more, whenever the thought of the pimp cuckold husband, Trevor, crossed his mind, his manhood throbbed harder. He was passionately aroused by the act of taking his distant brother's most prized possession, his wife Theodora.

After 45 minutes of riding the gigantic erection, Theodora was delirious; she had already climaxed multiple times and the stud under her was still continuing fucking her brains out.

Investigating his eyes, Theodora discovered an animalistic lust as Jordan gritted his teeth bellowed. Soon she sensed cock head of the shaft ramming her womanhood expand and the balls boiling under her married pussy. Stream after stream of intense hot cum burned her womb and cervix. She yelled at the electrifying sensation shuddering like a dry leaf as her hands were unable to muffle her groans. Jordan violated her juicy lips kissing her in lust while she kissing back him in gratitude for the amorous delight he had given her.

After they finished, surges of white cum spilled out of the conservative mother's freshly fucked womanhood as her bosoms were marked with love bites from the potent stud.

The first light of the morning began to pour in from the open window and Carolina got up stretching her arms. She breathed in the fresh air of the morning as her mind got crowded with the illicit adventures of the last night. She looked around and sensed she was still in bed with Dominic, who was resting oblivious to the entire world. She rapidly got up and pulled his shirt over her naked body as she opened the door. Noah was relaxing on the couch, but perhaps not likely as he would have in his own bed.

Carolina sat beside him and caressed his hairs. Noah gradually opened his eyes and saw his gorgeous wife alongside him. Her hairs were disheveled and she was wearing a baggy shirt. He understood whose shirt it was and where from she was coming. Moreover, her cheeks, neck, and lips bore the love bites of her ardent lover. Carolina kissed him on the forehead and greeted him, "Good morning love! I love you so much."

"I love you too sweetheart. Please let's go home now," Noah literally begged as he embraced her in his warmth.

"Yes, my love! Let's go home!" Carolina kissed his lips and acknowledged.

Erik and Beth

Erik and Beth sat together, watching the scene unfold on the TV in front of them. They'd been married for 2 years, and had started watching hardcore porn together about a month before to jazz up their sex lives a bit.

There were two men and a woman having sex, and Beth was mesmerized. They had seen this in several other movies, but in this one the men were bi-sexual. They alternated between fucking the woman, and sucking on each other's cocks.

Beth asked, "What do you think of that honey? You don't see that everyday."

"And I don't want to see that everyday, it didn't say anything about this on the box when I rented it."

Beth's hand slid into her panties, she found she was getting very wet.

"It looks exciting, we should try it," she teased. "I have a friend at work who everyone says is bi, I could ask him over."

"Maybe you could call your girlfriend Joanne over instead," replied Erik. "I think that you just want to try a three way, from what everyone says Joanne would be more than willing."

Beth laughed as Erik inserted his own hand into her now damp panties and let his fingers explore. She looked at the bodies on the screen and tried to imagine Erik and herself with another man. Erik's fingers found her clit, and she suddenly found herself shuddering to an orgasm.

"Uh, oh God, FUCK YES," she cried as Erik rubbed her harder. She ground her pussy against his hand and rode out the sensations that ran through her body. She collapsed against him and sighed, a smile played on her face.

"Well that was a surprise!" said Erik. "What's gotten into you?"

"I've just been horny all day babe," she lied. "Now I just want to suck on your dick," she said as she quickly pulled his underwear off. Taking his cock into her mouth she found herself thinking about the scene in the movie, and vowed to make it happen in real life. As Erik started to cum, her plan started to take form.

Erik had always been devoted to her, and why not? She stood 5' 11" tall, had a lean body that was sculpted by aerobics, and long flowing chestnut hair. She loved sex, and the two of them did it as often as possible. She knew that he wanted to have a three way with her and another woman, and she was open to that. The problem was to find a way to get him to have it with another man. "Enter, Joanne," she thought.

Joanne was Beth's best friend. They did a lot together; they shopped, went to the gym, and played tennis. Beth knew that Joanne was bi-sexual, but she had never tried anything with her, their relationship was platonic. She nervously dialed her number, knowing this was the biggest favor she would ever ask of anyone.

When Joanne heard the plan she quickly agreed. Erik had always interested her; he kept himself in great shape and had an easygoing personality that appealed to her. She could hardly believe that Beth had asked her to seduce him. They set it up for Friday of that week.

Beth hung up the phone and took a deep breath. Her pussy was tingling and she lay down on the bed and smiled as she touched herself. She found herself getting very wet at the thought of her plan, and the image of Erik and Joanne fucking bought her swiftly to orgasm.

That Friday night Beth called Erik and said she would be late getting home from work, but that Joanne would be stopping by. She asked him to entertain her until she got home. Erik agreed, telling her they would watch a movie or something until she got ther e .

Joanne arrived a few minutes later, lugging her gym bag. Erik let her in and asked how she was.

"I'm fine, but I really need a shower. I just had a great workout and I didn't feel like showering at the gym. Is it ok if I do it here?"

"No problem," replied Erik. You know where it is, holler if you need anything."

Joanne smiled and headed up to the bathroom. She quickly stripped and started the hot water running. A couple minutes later she called down "Erik? Erik, are you there? Can you bring me a towel? I haven't got mine with me."

Erik went upstairs and grabbed a towel from the closet. He knocked on the bathroom door and said "I'll just leave it here by the door."

"Can you bring it in to me? I've got soap in my eye and I don't want to trip."

Erik opened the door and tried not to look, but couldn't help it. Joanne was out of the shower and stood there completely nude, and dripping wet. The water glistened on her small but perfectly rounded breasts, her nipples were swollen and erect. He looked lower and could see that her pussy was completely shaved.

"Oh," said Joanne, "I guess you've seen me naked now. I'm sure Beth won't mind, she's seen me lots of times at the gym. Say, I'm a little sore from working out, would you mind drying my back for me?"

Erik couldn't pull his eyes from that delectable looking twat. "Um, ok, I guess."

He stepped behind her and started to gently pat the water from her with the towel. When her back was done she turned and said "You may as well dry my front too, after all, you've seen everything already."

Erik took a deep breath and continued to dry Joanne. He ran the towel over her tits, feeling the hardness of her nipples. She sat back on the vanity and lifted her right leg, lewdly displaying herself.

"Can you just dry my pussy for me too? It seems to be extra wet, I can't put my panties on like this."

Erik stared at the hairless piece of heaven in front of him, his cock already at full hardness. He looked down and saw that his sweatpants were wet at the tip of his straining dick. Joanne looked and saw it too.

"Oh dear, are you ok Erik? I didn't mean to excite you like this, I mean, your not going to get blue balls or anything, are you?"

"Um, I'll be ok, I'm really sorry. Sometimes my cock has a mind of it's own."

"Well, Beth won't be home for a while…do you want me to take care of that for you? I'm actually kind of horny myself; I haven't been with anyone in a while. I'd really appreciate it if you would let me finish what I started."

She gazed into Erik's eyes with a look of open lust. She

knew it was all over for him right there. Stepping forward she got on tiptoes to kiss him, one hand slipped behind his back to pull him closer, the other cupped this hard cock.

They quickly went into the bedroom; Joanne climbed onto the bed and got on all fours with her head down on a pillow.

"Fuck me from behind Erik, that's how I like it. Just shove it in now, I'm so hot for you my cunt just has to have you now."

Erik quickly obliged, he pulled off his sweatpants and mounted her from the rear. His need was urgent, he buried his cock as deeply as he could, Joanne so wet that he slid in easily. With one hand he reached under her and played with her nipples. Joanne cri e d out with pleasure, and reached her hand down to play with his balls as he fucked her.

"What the fuck is going on!?" Beth was standing in the doorway surveying the scene in front of her. "Erik, what are you doing!?!?!"

Erik pulled out of Joanne, his departure accompanied by a loud "Slurrrppp" from the wetness of their fucking.

"Beth, I thought you were going to be late. I, um, I was helping Joanne with a towel, and, well, fuck, I'm really sorry honey. I didn't mean for this to happen.

Joanne rolled over and winked at Beth. "It was my fault Beth, please don't blame Erik. He's just a man, you know how they are."

Beth looked at Erik, he winced from how mad she looked.

"Please don't hate me honey, I'll do anything you say. I'm really sorry."

That's what Beth was waiting to hear. "You'll do anything!? What the fuck do you think can make up for you fucking my best friend?"

"I don't know! Anything you want."

"All right then Mr. Two-timer. I have an idea for how you can make this up to me. I want you to see how it feels for me to get fucked by another man. Not only that, your going to do whatever I tell you to do while I'm fucking him. Any questions?"

Erik looked stunned, but there was nothing he could do. He just said "Ok, whatever you want honey."

Beth walked over to the phone and quickly dialed while Erik and Joanne watched. She covered the mouthpiece as she talked, Erik couldn't hear what she said. She hung up and looked to Erik again.

That was my friend from work, Greg. He'll be over in 10 minutes; he's always wanted to fuck me so now he's going to get his wish.

"Do you want me to stay? I feel bad, I kind of started this whole thing," said Joanne.

"Sure," replied Beth. "It's not really your fault, I blame Erik and now he's going to pay for it."

Erik couldn't say anything. Beth told him to sit on the bed and wait for his punishment.

A few minutes later the doorbell rang and Beth ran down to answer it. She came back into the bedroom, followed by Greg. He was about 6 foot tall, brown hair and looked lean and muscular.

"Erik, this is Greg. He's the one I mentioned before. You remember, the bi-sexual one. Here's the deal – I'm too pissed off to get horny right now so I'm going to need something to put me in the mood. I think you giving Paul a blowjob will go a long way towards getting me ready. Paul, why don't you strip so that we can get started?"

Paul quickly pulled off his clothes. He stood in front of the three of them, his cock hanging flaccid.

Beth sat on the bed with Joanne, and told Erik to kneel down in front of Paul. He slowly obeyed.

"Now, I want you to reach out with your tongue and lick the tip of his cock."

Erik looked back at Beth, a pleading look in his eye. She responded with an arched eyebrow and said, "Well, what are you waiting for? It's got to get hard before it can fuck me, make it hard."

Erik looked back to the cock hanging in front of him. With a feeling of defeat, he extended his tongue out and gently licked the head of it. "Not to bad," he thought. Hopefully this will go fast." He licked again, and Greg's cock began to respond, growing fatter and longer with each subsequent touch of Erik's tongue.

"That's it, your getting it hard now," said Beth. "I'm

going to make you my cocksucking bitch, that's what you get for fucking Joanne."

"Why don't you make him suck the whole thing now," asked Joanne. "It's nice and hard, have him take it all in his mouth. He should know how to suck it, I'm sure he's learned how to do it from all the times you've blown him."

"Joanne's right Erik, suck his cock now, just like I've always done for you."

Greg's cock was at full attention now, and pre-cum started to leak from the tip. Erik took a deep breath and parted his lips, just allowing the head to slip into his mouth. The pre-cum made it slide over his lips, and his tongue caressed the head as he started to suck. Greg carefully held Erik's head, and with a groan he slid fully into Erik's mouth and started to slowly fuck in and out.

After about a minute of this Greg was surprised to feel Erik's hand come up between his legs and touch his balls. He moaned, and spread his legs a bit so that Erik would have easier access. Erik's hand played with each ball, one at a time, feeling the weight of each and gently massaging them. Greg moaned louder, he was getting close.

"Look at that!" said Joanne. "Erik's got his hard-on back! Looks like someone is enjoying his punishment."

"Erik!" exclaimed Beth, "What's going on? I'm going to have to come up with other ways to punish you if you enjoy this too much."

Erik released Greg's cock from his mouth, and sat back. He looked down at his cock, which was fully aroused and freely leaking pre-cum. He shyly said to Beth "I'm sorry babe, I didn't realize I could get excited by sucking on a cock."

"Well, lets see if you get excited watching your wife get fucked then. Get over here and undress me."

Erik got up and walked to the bed, his cock waving in

front of him. Beth stood and allowed him to remove her clothes. As he did, Joanne kept reaching out and touching his dick, spreading his wetness up and down the shaft, and onto his balls.

Once she was undressed, Beth asked, "Now, how were you fucking Joanne? Wasn't she on all fours on the bed, with you behind her? I think that's how you should watch Greg fucking me, but you should have a better view. Lay down on your back on the bed, with y o ur head at the edge."

Erik did as he was told, and Beth climbed over him so that her pussy hovered above his face, her legs on either side of him and her head over his cock. She looked over her shoulder at Greg and said, "Fuck me now."

Greg stepped up behind her, that beautiful ass offered up for his glistening cock. He took hold of her hips, and wiped his wet dick up and down her labia lips. She was already quite wet, and Erik lying beneath them watched as his wife's pussy spread and Gr e g's freshly sucked cock slowly slid inside her.

Joanne came around the other side of the bed, and knelt down, legs on either side of Erik and looked into Beth's eyes. She leaned forward and kissed her deeply, Beth responded by slipping her tongue into her mouth. Joanne reached down and found Erik's soaking cock, guided it to her bare pussy, and sat down on it. It went in easily, she was very wet from viewing all the activity.

Erik moaned deeply as he felt Joanne settle down on top of him. He was carefully watching Greg's cock slide in and out of Beth's pussy, he could smell the aroma of their fucking.

"Erik, I want you to lick Greg's balls when his cock is fully in me, and as he pulls out I want you to lick his shaft. Do it good, remember, you're my little cocksucking bitch."

Joanne giggled at this, and bounced up and down on his cock a bit. "You tell him, Beth. He's lucky you let him suck cocks anyway, especially ones that have been in your cunt."

Erik started earnestly licking Greg's cock as he fucked Beth. As Greg plunged in fully, Erik sucked on his balls, taking them fully in his mouth. When he pulled out, he released his balls and fervently licked his shaft. He could taste both Beth's pussy jui c e s, and Greg's cock juices with each stroke. He licked Beth's clit, and she squealed and kissed Joanne urgently.

Beth started rocking back and forth, meeting Greg's thrusts. "I'm getting close, but I don't want you to cum Erik. I just want you to watch. Uhhh, God that's good." Greg ground deeply into her and Beth groaned louder, "UHHHH, fuck, it's so fucking good! Can you see my cunt getting fucked Erik? OHHHH, fuck, God it's so good, fuck, FUCK FUCK FUCK, I'm CUMMING NOW!" she screamed as Greg roughly grabbed her hips and buried his cock as deeply as he could. Her body shook violently, and she sobbed as Joanne grabbed a nipple with each hand and gently squeezed.

Greg exploded deep in her pussy, announcing it with a cry of release. He bucked against her, his balls clenching as his cum filled her. Greg lay beneath them, gazing at the spectacle of their amazing orgasms.

"Don't pull out Greg, keep fucking me until your cock

is soft," said Beth. Greg obliged, and continued to slowly fuck in and out, as his cock slowly lost its hardness. Erik, lay there watching the deflating cock make a gooey mess of his wife's cunt, and wondered what she had in mind.

Finally, he could enter her no more, and he slid free of her pussy. Greg stepped back, and Beth rolled off of Erik. Joanne had been slowly fucking him, careful not to let him cum, and she too dismounted.

Beth looked at Greg's cock and said, "Look at that. It's all covered with cum, and it's not hard at all anymore. I think we need to do something about it, don't you Joanne?"

"Yes, I definitely agree. I'd like to have that fucking me, but it definitely needs to be cleaned and re-excited. But, what can we do? I'm certainly not going to put that nasty cock in my mouth."

"Well, how about we have my little cocksucking bitch do it for us? That way we can just relax and watch.

Greg, I have another job for you," Beth said with a sadistic smile. "I want you to clean up the nasty mess we made of poor Greg's cock, and I want you to get it hard again so that Joanne can fuck it. Greg, why don't you lay down on the bed?"

Greg lay back on the bed, his knees bent and spread, his dripping cock exposed. Erik got on the bed too, his own cock dripping from fucking Joanne, and aching for release.

"If you clean that up well enough, I might let you cum later," said Beth. "Now, I want you to kiss that dick, make out with it and lick off all that cum. Make sure you get the balls nice and clean too."

Erik made himself comfortable between Greg's legs, and started to kiss and lick the cum from his cock. He took the limp shaft in his mouth and strongly sucked, tasting the after effects of their fucking. He licked his balls, and as the whole cock became cl e a n, it also started to respond and grow hard again.

Beth and Joanne stood watching, almost hypnotized with lust at the sight of Erik so willingly performing and enjoying such lewdness. Joanne reached between Beth's thighs and felt wetness running down them.

"You've got cum running out of your pussy Beth, do you want me to get that for you?" she asked. "Erik seems to be enjoying clean up duty so much, maybe I should try."

Beth quickly lay down beside Greg and said, "So you want to clean up cum too? Well, that makes you my nasty little cunt eating bitch, now get to work." She lay the same way as Greg, her knees bent and her pussy displayed, cum was plastered in and out of her, and now that she was on her back it started to run down the crack of her ass.

Joanne smiled and dove in, her face coming down onto her friend's well-fucked twat. Her tongue darted in and out of her, tasting and cleaning up the cum. Beth grabbed her head with both hands and pushed Joanne's face into her pussy even harder. She involuntarily ground her hips around as Joanne sucked, she groaned with pleasure as her friend grabbed her ass to help her grind.

Erik looked up from Greg to see his wife being eaten out by Joanne. The sight of it made his cock grow even harder, although he would have thought that impossible. His cock was completely coated in pre-cum, and it dripped off of him onto the bed. He licked his lips, savoring the last of Greg's cum.

"Greg's cock is all clean and hard again," he said to his writhing wife.

"Greg," Beth said between gasps, "Why don't you fuck my cunt eating bitch from behind while she eats me. Erik, you can play with yourself while you watch."

Greg quickly got behind Joanne and entered her. Joanne let out a muffled moan as she felt her pussy filled, and sucked even harder on Beth's delicious cunt. Erik ran his fingers from the tip of his cock down to the base of his balls as he viewed the debauchery. He was extremely excited, and he was finding it hard not to cum.

After a few minutes of fucking, Joanne started to quiver and make sounds like she was going to cum. Beth was pushing her face hard into her pussy, and when Joanne started to shake, she released her head and grabbed her nipples, the same way Joanne had teas e d hers. Joanne raised her head and shouted "Oh fucking GOD, I'M CUMMING SO FUCKING HARD RIGHT FUCKING NOW!!!"

Greg had hold of her by the hips, and plunged in and out for all he was worth. He felt his balls rise up, and he let go another load in Joanne's cunt. He cried out and collapsed, exhausted from his second orgasm.

Joanne rolled off of Beth, and Beth looked over at Erik, who was still playing with his extremely wet cock.

"Lay down Erik," she said, "It's your turn to be the cunt eating bitch."

Erik lay back on the bed, and Beth helped Joanne position herself over his face. Erik looked up to see Joanne's bald pussy covered with cum lowering itself onto his face. It looked like Greg had exploded both inside and outside of her. "How could one guy h a ve that much cum?" he thought. Joanne sighed as she felt his tongue reach up to lick her smooth pussy. She reached down and pulled her lips apart, letting a big drop of cum fall from her into Erik's mouth. "Oh, that was nasty," said Beth. "That makes me w a nt to fuck his cock while he sucks on you."

Beth straddled Erik and took hold of his cock. She guided it to her pussy lips, and as she impaled herself on it, Joanne lowered herself and sat on his face. Erik let out a stifled cry of pleasure.

Beth rocked back and forth, her eyes closed as she toyed with her nipples. Joanne rode Erik's face, wiping her wet slit all over him. Soon, Erik started to groan and Beth felt his cock jerking inside her cunt.

"He's cumming Joanne, grind your pussy into his face harder!" Joanne did and Erik's whole body started to involuntarily jerk as he released his load into Beth. He felt someone start licking his balls, and knew that Greg was returning the favor he had given him.

Erik, sated at last, went limp and lay under Joanne. Both Joanne and Beth rolled off, and Greg ran his tongue up his cock, savoring the juices. Erik quivered and smiled.

Beth looked down at her pussy and said, "Uh oh, I'm all messy again. Looks like I have one more job for you Erik, and then I think I'll forgive you for fucking Joanne."

Joanne and Greg helped Beth into position over Erik, who was exhausted but still more than willing to eat his wife out. As she lowered her sloppy cunt down and felt his tongue enter her, she sighed thinking things had worked out even better than she planned them.

Joanne said, "Hey, you've forgiven him for fucking me, but what if he does it again? You never know, he might try the same thing again."

Beth swiveled her hips in a circular motion on Erik's

face and said "Well, if that were to happen then I think I'd make him into my little cocksucking cunt-eating bitch again. How does next Friday sound to you guys?" she said with a laugh.

The MILF and Her Cuckolding Husband

I wasn't usually one to surprise David at work, but then he usually didn't spend so much time at the office. In reality, it was David who usually surprised me at lunch time, swinging home for an impromptu quickie when the mood struck, which was frequently. "How am I supposed to make it through the salt mines all day without my fix?" he'd say, coming up behind me, lifting my skirt, sliding his hand down my lacy panties. He worked hard and played hard. But lately he'd only been working hard. I needed my fix, as well.

"I brought you lunch!" I said, strutting into my husband David's office in my tight skirt and kitten heels, picnic basket full of goodies in my hand. I wasn't usually one to surprise David at work--but then he usually didn't spend so much time at the office. In reality, it was David who usually surprised me at lunch time, swinging home for an impromptu quickie when the mood struck, which was frequently.

"How am I supposed to make it through the salt mines all day without my fix?" he'd say, coming up behind me, lifting my skirt, sliding his hand down my lacy panties.

He worked hard and played hard. But lately he'd only been working hard. I needed my fix, as well.

This year we would be celebrating our 20th anniversary. We had always been the envy of our friends. David made an excellent salary, we had a beautiful house that I kept, and even after all of these years, we were always the couple that would sneak off to some dark corner to neck like teenagers--we couldn't keep our hands off each other. And it was no wonder: He'd aged wonderfully, only becoming more chiseled over time, his salt and pepper hair still thick, his physique strong and capable. And I knew he was still enamored with my 45 year old body, my hair still dark, save for one silver streak framing my face, my high cheek bones becoming more prominent with age, with only some subtle crows feet betraying me--crow's feet he would kiss lovingly and adoringly. My body, too, was holding up miraculously, my breasts still full, my ass still firm, my tummy still flat. Perhaps it was because we'd never had any kids. It's not that we didn't like children--but we liked fucking on the living room floor on a whim a lot more.

But we hadn't fucked on the living room floor or anywhere else in two months--an eternity for us. I knew it couldn't be that I'd become unattractive--I was still deflecting advances from every man who came my way on a daily basis. No, he simply had a big project at work that was taking all of his time and draining him of all of his energy. But, being an excellent wife, I knew that meant he would need a pick me up more than ever. So I went to his office with my picnic basket to give him a good meal, and then a little peep show to remind him why it was a good idea to come home from time to time.

But he didn't look happy to see me when I went into his office unannounced. He was sitting at his desk, and when he saw me, a look of sheer horror came across his face. "It's not a good time, Jessica," he said. "I'm really very busy right now. But I'll be home early for dinner! You should run along!"

"Nonsense," I countered, hopping up on his desk with ease and crossing my legs coquettishly. "You can't be expected to work on an empty stomach, and if I know you, you haven't even thought about eating yet today--you get so focused on your work. But I know you're hungry." I unbuttoned my shirt casually as I spoke to him and let it hang open, no bra, my breasts hanging above him as I perched on his desk.

He looked me up and down and said, "Oh, god..."

" You forgot what you were missing, didn't you darling?" I pulled a finger sandwich out of the picnic basket and fed it to him.

"Listen, honey, you really have to go. I'm sorry--but

you know what a little shit Jason is. Ever since he took over he's trying to prove he's a man by cracking the whip." Jason was the new CEO. He had succeeded his late father to the position, but at only 24, he had a lot to prove. For people like my poor husband, his rise had been infuriating. He was only a kid, lacking any experience. David hated him. "You can't be in here right now. Besides, I can't risk that little piss-ant walking in here and seeing your gorgeous tits. Those are all mine. So, please--run along home. I'll be there early, I promise."

"I don't like being rejected like this," I said, annoyed. It never occurred to me that he'd be anything other than happy to have me come by--it certainly never occurred to me that he wouldn't want me showing off my tits. Was this it? Had we finally reached the point where I was just his wife--not a sexual being? But still, even as these thoughts ran through my head, I maintained my composure. I wouldn't overreact until I had a real reason to.

So, I bent down to kiss him goodbye, ever the attentive wife, and that's when I saw it: A woman's hand coming from under his desk, pressing into the floor. "What the..." I knelt down for a better look.

"No, Jessica, don't!" but it was too late. I saw her. There, on all fours, was Carmen, my husband's new intern, no top, her flat chest exposed, my husband's cum dribbling down her chin.

"Well, I'm sorry to interrupt," I said evenly, but my blood was running cold, my mind swimming "Don't mind me, I'll get out of your way."

"Jessica, wait--I can explain!" David was following me.

"There isn't any explanation," I went for the door.

"Jessica--please! It's not a big deal!"

It's not a big deal? I catch him giving his cock to some moronic little flat-chested girl and it's not a big deal?

"You'll be sorry, you son of a bitch," I said, slamming the door as I left, though even I wasn't sure just what I meant by that.

I rushed onto the elevator, needing to get as far away as David as I possibly could. The full gravity of it was too much for me to bear, and I was in a kind of shock. Everything seemed slow motion--calm and distant, like being underwater. There was a rushing in my ears, and I could hear my own pounding heart--but the beat was slow and steady.

One floor down and there was Jason, CEO, my

husband's nemesis. It was easy to see why he'd be such a hated figure: Not only was he the man in charge of everything when he was too young to have possibly earned it, he was also breathtakingly handsome. He was the kind of man who had always gotten what he wanted and always would. It was a hated position I sympathized, having always been that kind of woman. That is until now.

"Mrs. Savage!" said Jason, warmly. He was genuinely nice on top of everything else. What an asshole. "So nice to see you! Stopping in to see David?"

"I...yes, I was." The world was continuing on as normal, in spite of what I'd just seen. How could that be?"

"You know, I tell David all of the time what a lucky man he is to have you," Jason smiled.

"Oh, you think so?" Tears started to spring to my eyes, now, involuntarily. Though standing beside me, Jason didn't know it.

"We all think so. I wish you'd come by more often! Seeing you around the office is good for morale," he turned to me give me a cute little wink, but when he saw my face his smile faded into a look of concern. "Mrs. Savage, what's wrong?"

"I--" I was stopped by the sudden realization of what a handsome, attentive boy I had in front of me. His blue eyes were looking deep into mine with caring and concern, and it occurred to me for the first time that he had a little crush on me--that he had always been overly attentive with me at the office parties, keeping me in his line of sight at all times, looking me up and down appreciatively. And here he was, so genuinely wanting to help me when he felt I was in distress. "I...it's...I'm sorry. Yes, I'm fine," I finally answered him. "My...my aunt passed away this morning. We were very close. I came here to see if David could take a little time to comfort me, but he was so deep in his...project...I told didn't bring it up," I hoped he wouldn't question the lie, and he didn't. I couldn't bring myself to admit to this gorgeous young man that I'd been tossed aside for someone younger.

Rather, he said, "Well, I've got a little time. Is there anything I can do?"

"Yes," I answered. "Yes, I think there is."

I took him back to the house. He agreed to take the afternoon off and keep me company. I told him what I really needed was a distraction. I asked him to talk to me about anything other than my aunt--this would allow me to avoid the subject I'd lied about, and also gave me a chance to get to know him a little bit. I fixed us each a drink.

"No...no, I don't have a girlfriend," he blushed when I asked him about his love life. It was surprising--a young, handsome, rich boy so shy about the subject of girls. I found it adorable. "The truth is...I've never really had time for a girlfriend. Gosh, I haven't had a girlfriend since the 9th grade. And that was just for two weeks."

"You're kidding?" I was truly fascinated. How was it possible girls weren't throwing themselves at him right in left? "But then, I suppose you enjoy playing the field," I answered my own question.

"There isn't really much of a field. I've spent my entire life in my dad's office. When other kids were at parties and joining clubs, I was here. Most of the people who work at the company have known me since I was a kid, and they still think of me that way."

"Well, you appear to be a man, now," I smiled, my drink warming me up.

"I actually...I've had a more sheltered life than most people realize."

"Jason," I was beginning to catch on to what he was telling me, "--have you ever been with a girl?"

His face turned beet red at the question. "I mean...there's been some kissing..."

I downed my drink. This was too much! He was an honest to God virgin! "Finish your drink--I'll get you another one."

"I should probably get back to the office, soon..." he said nervously.

"No, you shouldn't. You should stay here and keep me company," I said, handing him a drink. It was then that I realized he had an erection--and an enormous one at that. It was hard to keep my eyes off of, until he saw me staring and went to cover it with his hands. "No, no--don't be embarrassed," I said, pulling his hands back, and then letting my hand rest in his for just a moment before pulling away. "I'm...flattered, actually. I...I haven't been feeling very attractive, lately."

"Are you kidding?" Jason laughed, incredulously. "I don't know how that's possible--you're beautiful."

"My husband doesn't seem to think so, anymore," I blurted out. My drink was getting to me.

"I don't know if I should be hearing about your marital pro--"

"No, but you might want to hear this," I continued, the truth tumbling out in an unstoppable tidal wave. "I wasn't upset earlier because of my aunt. I was upset because when I went into David's office, that fucking adorable little Carmen, was sucking his cock."

"What?"

"Hiding under the desk with his cum on her mouth--I'm sorry--I know I shouldn't be saying this--you're his boss, I shouldn't be jeopardizing his job like that..." and I meant it--that was not what I had intended. "Please, don't fire him. Goddamnit, I shouldn't have told you..."

"He cheated on you? On you?" He was livid. But he didn't seem to care at all that David had been carrying on with an intern at work. No, he was livid because he'd hurt me. How could those boy care so much and my very own husband care so little? "He has no idea....he has no idea..." Jason started babbling.

"He has no idea what?'

"He has no idea how jealous I've always been that he has you! How could he even dream of being with someone else? If I had the chance to touch your body, I'd never stop touching it."

We were both standing, now, eyeing each other, panting. The air between us was electric. I looked down and saw his hard-on was raging.

I walked slowly up to him, put my hand to his chest, and

backed up him up to his chair until he was sitting.

" Do you mean that?" I asked, kneeling down, unzipping his pants.

"Yes," he said nervously, as I tugged them off.

"Because I need to be fucked so badly by someone who appreciates me. Do you understand? I need it..." I grabbed the band of his boxer briefs and tugged them off, unleashing him. I couldn't believe my eyes--it was enormously thick and long--the biggest I'd ever seen, and David had been more than adequate in that department. "Oh my god...do you even know what a beautiful cock you have?" I asked, and he blushed, boyishly. "Will you stroke it for me? I want to watch you stroke it"

"I don't know if this is right..." he said, but he trailed off as I stood up before him and took off my shirt. His mouth was open as he stared at my dark, pert nipples. His hand instinctively went to his cock and started stroking. I unzipped my skirt and wriggled out of it.

"Don't stroke so fast! That's it, good boy. My god, that cock is so eager," I said as I tugged at my lace thong and pulled it up between my pussy lips, letting the wet lace rub against my clit.

"You have to stop, or I'm never going to last..." he

said, visibly sweating.

" Shhh...calm down, baby. I'm going to help you. We're going to help each other." I knelt down before him, took his hand off of his cock and placed them on the arms of the chair. I slowly started licking the head of his enormous cock, holding it up gently with two hands. "You're going to fuck me all night long with this thing. But first, we have to build up your tolerance. Now, if you feel close, you're going to pull my hair to let me know. Understand?" I started taking him into my mouth as he groaned, but it was difficult fit his enormous girth in my mouth. I was stretched to capacity, but I was determined to take as much of him down as I could. He went past my tongue, touched the back of my throat, and I gagged, my throat contracting on his cock. I felt a sharp pain as he tugged my hair a little too hard, and I pulled off of him. He was panting hard.

"You are eager. We're going to give your cock a little break. So, no touching!" I instructed. You're not going to touch that cock until I tell you to.

"So I'm just going to sit here?"

"Not at all." I pulled him toward me by the legs until he was leaning back in the arm chair. I stood up, swung my long, toned leg over him, and stood, straddling him.

I lowered myself down and sat not not on his cock, but on his stomach, his cock behind me. I leaned forward and said, "Put your mouth on my breast."

He leaned forward like a good boy and started licking my nipple. He was a natural. His tongue was strong and responsive. As my nipple grew harder, so did the strokes of his tongue. He began to suck gently, and I moaned as I started grinding my pussy into his rock hard abs. He sucked harder and I leaned back, him leaning with me, and I let my long dark, silver streaked hair drape over his cock and bulbous balls, tickling him. He bucked a bit. "Easy...easy..." I instructed. "You've got a long way to go."

He pulled his mouth from my breast and cradled me in his muscular arms as he looked me over. I had a moment of self-consciousness--I was much older than he was. I hadn't turned the lights out, I shouldn't let him look so close. My hand went to cover my lower tummy, but he moved my hand behind my back. "Don't cover a thing," he said. "I want to see everything." He slid two fingers into my pussy like a pro, and the feel of his thick hands made me more wet than I'd been in years. "Is that right? Do you like that," he asked.

"Yes...." I moaned, feeling my muscles contract. "Just like that. How does my pussy feel to you?"

"So wet...you're dripping down my hand...it feels....God, your pussy feels strong..."

I laughed. It wasn't a description I'd expected but I liked it. My pussy is strong, I repeated to myself as I squeezed his fingers with my cunt. He groaned as though I'd done the same thing to his cock. "Do you want to feel my pussy wrapped around your cock?" I asked.

"Oh, God, yes..." he moaned.

"Come with me," I instructed, leading him into the bedroom.

I got up on the bed, leaned back and spread my legs wide. "Look at my cunt," I said. "Tell me what you see."

He took his thick fingers and opened my lips like a present. He looked hungry, enraptured as he looked into me. "It's perfect..." he said.

"Taste it," I commanded. He licked his lips, bent down, and breathed me in deeply. He looked like he was in heaven taking in my scent. Then he kissed my pussy--a deep, slow french kiss, tonguing me sweetly, deeply, as he explored.

"Good boy...Mmmm...how are you so good at this?" It

was incredible--it was devoid of technique or tricks. He was letting his longing for me guide him and he was the better for it.

"You're so responsive…" he said into my mound. "I'm following your lead."

"What's my pussy telling you?"

"This little nub gets harder when I lick it…" he said, flicking my clit.

"Mmm-hmmm….what else?"

"And the more I lick it your nub, the more you gush right here…" he said, putting his fingers inside of me as he began sucking hard on my clit. I moaned loudly and he slid his finger in and out quickly as he flicked my nub and sucked me into ecstasy.

"Jason…" I moaned.

"What an idiot his is…" he said into my cunt. "I would do anything to please you…" He dug his tongue in, and without instruction, he explored further and further down, pushing my legs back, exposing my asshole. He looked into it for a moment, then plunged his tongue in deeply, without hesitation.

"Oh my God, yes…"

"Is that okay?"

"Yes, my God! Don't stop...please..." I thought I'd be teaching him, but now I was ready to follow his lead, let him take control of my body.

"I love the way you taste," he said. "I'm never going to stop licking you..." he ran his hands up my body and grabbed my tits as he buried his face deeply into my ass, sucking and licking as I squirmed. His hands moved back down, and he spread my cheeks as far as they would go, then dug his long tongue into my tight little cave.

I heard a key in the door, but Jason didn't seem to, so focused was he on the task at hand. He withdrew his tongue, and said, "I have to fuck you...Mrs. Savage, I have to fuck you..."

"Yes....yes, I want you to." I knew damn well my husband would be walking in any minute. I grabbed his cock and guided it to my pussy. It was so thick, it felt like a fist pressing up against me. But I spread my legs as far as they would go and said, "Don't be gentle. Press into me."

He thrust hard, and I cried out loudly, adding, "Keep going! Keep going!" until he was all the way inside of me, down to the base.

"My God, Jason...."

"It's so hot and tight..." he said. His face was turning red.

"No matter what happens, don't stop--don't cum yet!" I growled. He began thrusting into me, unselfconsciously moaning as he did, and I sung out right back He filled me up--his cock was magnificent, transforming me into a primal beast. I wanted that fat cock to plug me up every which way. I wanted him everywhere. I wanted to him to fill me up. I wanted my husband to see he was pathetic compared to the men I could be having.

"What's that yelling?" David called out, coming up the stairs to our bedroom. I worried Jason would stop, but he only thrust harder, his heavy sack pounding against me rhythmically. In one fell swoop, he turned me over, spread my ass wide, and plunged his cock into my tight--and until that moment--virgin asshole. David had always wanted to, but for some reason I held back with him. Now Jason and I had both been each other's' firsts, and I let him tear me open happily, even encouraging him, "Faster, deeper, I want more of you...." And as the door to the bedroom opened, I was instructing Jason to fuck me harder, harder, harder...

I watched David's face as if in slow motion. His eyes were glued to Jason's cock, far more impressive than his own, entering his wife's sweet, devoted ass, over and over again.

"What the hell are you doing? Get off of her!" David yelled, starting towards Jason. But Jason shoved him to the ground with one hand, fucking me all the while.

"You love my cock more than his, don't you," Jason said to me. "You don't want his cock anymore, isn't that right?" My whole body was wild and bucking. I thought he may actually tear through me, his cock was so massive, but I didn't care--he could have his way with me.

"That's right," I said, and he groaned in pleasure as he thrust deeply and then held it there, both of us transfixed in the moment, panting, writhing, sighing.

"You don't have to do this!" David shouted from the floor, grabbing his hurt leg. He was helpless, laying on the floor, and with no choice but to watch us.

"Yes, I do...I need this young cock. My god...he doesn't let up..." I would have thought he'd cum long ago, inexperienced as he was, but he had incredible stamina. I vowed to myself I wouldn't stop until he did. I hadn't felt this wet and excited in ages, and I suddenly wondered how it was possible that just a few hours ago I'd gone skipping off to my husband's office in need of a cock that now seemed pathetic to me. Carmen-the-intern could have it--it was useless to me now.

"Jessica! Stop it!" he cried out, shrilly. God, he really was pathetic. I would have laughed right in his face, but Jason had his hands on my breasts, kneading them as he drove into me, and all I could do was sigh with guttural pleasure.

"I'm gonna kick your ass, Jason!" David tried to stand, but he fell down. Jason smacked my ass triumphantly and I arched my back. But then he surprised me. He withdrew his cock and my whole body cried out in protest. The thought of him leaving me unsatisfied was so cruel I couldn't bear it. He climbed off the bed and stroked his cock while he watched me.

"Tell David what you think of him," Jason instructed.

"I can't think of him at all," I answered, my hands reaching down to my soaking pussy, my fingers dug in, but they were like nothing compared to what I'd just experienced. "The only thing I can think about is how much I need you inside of me, again."

"You're just trying to hurt me, I know," David cut in, crying. He was actually crying! "Jessica, I'm so sorry-- but you don't have to do this!"

"Does it hurt, David? Does it hurt seeing someone else satisfy me?"

"Carmen didn't satisfy me! She's nothing compared

to you!"

"That's too bad, David," Jason said, a cruel smile on his face. "Because Carmen's all you've got now. You're not getting near your wife's body ever again. It belongs to me now."

David lunged towards Jason, enraged. But Jason was young and strong and fast, and it took nothing at all to floor David with just the back of his hand. He was sprawled out uselessly on the floor, but Jason wasn't taking any chances. He picked him up, set him down in the chair near my vanity, where the three way mirror reflected our bed. He tied him there with some scarves that were hanging nearby, binding his hands and feet. Finally, despite David's protests, Jason shoved a bunched-up scarf into David's mouth, and secured it with another. Bound and gagged and with nowhere to look but at the image of his wife moving on with a man less than half his age--David looked like the shell of a man that he truly was inside.

"Do you understand now that there's nothing you can do, David?" Jason taunted. It turned me on to see him becoming a man before my very eyes. "I always get what I want. And what I want is your wife." Tears came to David's eyes, but Jason wouldn't have it. "Don't give us that, now--you didn't want her a few hours ago! You took this incredible woman for granted! Jessica, baby--will you come here, please?" I scrambled over to him madly. I knelt before Jason's cock as David looked on. "Show David what he's never going to experience from you again."

At those words, I took him deeply and all at once down my throat. This time, he felt completely in control of the situation--I wasn't at all worried about his ability to hold out. So I sucked away at him with abandon, letting him slide down my throat, gagging me, and then all the way back up the to top, sucking his mushroom head tenderly before lunging back down again.

"My God, you are so good..." he moaned, and David winced. I cupped Jason's balls and gave them a gentle squeeze, sending him into a frenzy. He began face-fucking me deeply. I opened my throat to take him down, feeling as though I was drowning--but it was a great way to go.

"You are incredible..." he moaned. "I have to cum, Mrs. Savage...I'm going to cum..." Mrs. Savage. It turned me on to hear him call me that. To have him call me that in front of David.

"Please cum in my mouth, Jason," I looked him in the eyes, and he looked back into mine, before he threw back his head, let out a scream, and came harder than any man I'd ever encountered. A flood of cum rushing down my throat, filling my mouth, running down my chin.

"You bitch….how could you do this to me?" David was balling like a little bitch. But he didn't cry for me when Carmen had her lips around his pitiful cock. Did he really think it wouldn't bother me? Did he really think I'd take it lying down? Did he really think I was so pathetic that I would forgive him--as though I had no other options? And what were his options, now? How long would Carmen keep sucking his cock before she, too, moved on to someone better?

I swallowed down the rest of Jason's emission, hungrily, and went to lick my lips for the rest, but stopped. I looked at David, tied up, crying. I sauntered over, feeling more powerful than I ever had before.

"Poor baby. You didn't think you'd have to pay for your mistake, did you?" I said. "It hurts so badly, doesn't it? It hurt me, too. Seeing Carmen covered in your cum."

I leaned down and pulled the scarf off of his face, out of his mouth. "But then, I didn't know how good another person could taste." I said. "It tastes better than I ever imagined. It tastes better than you ever did. So I guess I forgive you."

With that I put my lips on his fiercely, one last kiss

goodbye. I pressed my cum covered tongue into his while he gagged. Pulling away I saw Jason's cream dripping off of David's mouth. "He tastes delicious, doesn't he? Maybe now you'll understand why I can never be with you again."

"Don't leave me--I'll never do it again!" he cried out.

"No, you won't. Because I won't be here. And it won't be long before Carmen sees you're past your prime, Grandpa," I smiled. "But some of us aren't." I picked up my clothes and took Jason's hand leading him towards the door. "Come on, Jason. I suspect you're ready to go again? And I want you to feel me pour all over you the way you poured yourself into me."

"You can't leave me here!" David cried.

"We'll untie you when we're done. Though, God knows when that will be," Jason smirked as he slapped my ass. I let out a girlish giggle and skipped down the stairs, the sound of David's sobs echoing after us.

The BDSM Community

Both were members of the local BDSM community within the region they lived in. They knew each other now for around a year. Both of them were married but not one to another. When they played as Dom and Sub, there was a spark between them but when they got out of those positions they were just friends, like everybody else on the facebook online club.

Having to travel to London for our annual BDSM club event where she will be playing a role together with her online friend at the London BDSM club which has been in operation for about 6 year now, but this was the first time she decided to go to an out - of-town party with him.

They'd just arrived back for the night at the hotel room. To save a little money, they had agreed to get one room with two beds. In different situations they both had been nude in front of each other; they should have no inhibitions to each other. He liked "leading" her to be nude and to do so many of the things she secretly fantasized about during their "scenes," but she felt a twinkle of combined fear and anticipation deep in the pit of her stomach tonight when he put the key in the door to the bed. This was the first time they were ever to be truly alone together.

She was 31 in the 4 "black studded high heels she was sporting, standing about 5'9" She had long dark brown hair which she highlighted as a blonde. She had milky white skin, which was quite a contrast to her fingernails and toenails matching the burgundy lipstick. She was dressed to conquer in fishnet stockings in a burgundy corset and black leather miniskirt, all of which had been off in the hours before while they played at the bar. He still insisted that she be completely naked during practice.

She was married but let her fetishes and dreams play out. Two of her only laws were no intimacy or private contact with married men whom partners did not know. It was a fair rule, leaving the door open to all sorts of other possibilities.

He was pretty tall, at least over 6', and very stunning. He is twenty years older than her. She used to like older men. All the older men she'd known in the past made her feel so safe and secure, and had a maturity level approaching her own. She quietly had a passion for "Daddy's" character-play, but never discussed anything with anyone she personally knew. The "taboo" subject matter had scared off too many people she knew. She found his very mischievous grin very attractive; part of her longed for him so much more. He was a mystery to her for the most part, he never really disclosed too much about himself to her and she never inquired. She loved playing the card of innocence, however she understood he was married and that his wife was not sure of his interest.

He opened the door and she followed him into the house, holding on the door handle the DO NOT DISTURB sign on. It was 1:30 am and both were tired from the club scene they were doing.

"Will you take a shower?" When she ripped the laces free from her corset, she told him. She marched over to him and lifted her arms telling him she needed his help to pull it off.

"Yeah, I think tonight I'm going to take a quick shower," he answered as he pulled the corset over her head.

"Alright," she walked back to her room, folded the corset, put it in her purse, and plopped it down onto her pillow.

He started to remove his belt and she just smiled at him. He grinned at her as he let down his pants to his knees. She gazed up and down at him; to her he seemed so yummy. Immediately she stood up, and walked to him. She perceived the need for him to remove his jacket. Silently she unbuttoned the top button and looked up to see what sort of expression he could have on his lips.

Grinning, he said, "Thank you." She blushed and looked back at the next button, and the next one, until all the buttons had been unfastened, then she slipped her palms over his chest and over his arms, down to his wrists. She then pressed her back against him, buried her face in his bare chest and deeply inhaled. She'd loved a man's fragrance. She stood there just for a few seconds, taking in his smell. She found herself dreaming about crossing the line she had set around married men, backed up, unbuttoned each of her sleeves ' cuffs and started removing her top. She took it to the wardrobe and had it hung up. She caught a glimpse of his naked ass when she stepped into the shower, then closed the door.

She went back to bed and put her right foot on the pillow, unbuckled her strap to her shoe and put it in her purse, and she did the same with her left shoe. She then unzipped and slid down her jacket, bent over at the knees while she removed her feet from it. Folding it carefully, she put it on top of the corset in her purse. Unhooking from her garter belt, she brought up each foot one by one on the bed and slipped it down her legs and off her feet. She did not understand that in such a beautiful manor she had to do it, nobody was listening, she just had to. Each time she dressed up like this it was her ritual. She then stripped off her thong too. Then she went completely naked beneath her sheets, turned off the lights and prepared for his shower to end. She just wanted to have a bath, particularly after the strength of the scene they did earlier in the night. Her body was tired and she needed a deep, calming and peaceful bath.

She must have wandered off because the bathroom door squeak made her hop about as far as the ceiling and let out a slight yelp. He crossed by, a towel around his neck, and by his bed turned the light on.

"Your turn?" She asked in the Light blinking.

"I didn't know that you also needed a shower, you could have followed me," he said with a smile.

"No Sir, I'd rather have a nice quiet bath." She replied as she got up with her own mischievous grin, took a little box out of her purse, and went to the bathroom.

She opened her package after closing the door, which had a few rose scented aromatherapy candles and a bottle of bath salts, with the same fragrance. She lit the candles and put one on each end of the mirror to show the light throughout the entire room, switched off the light and went and sat down on the side of the pool. She switched on the bath, temperature change and drain collection. She put in some of the salt at the bath and swirled it in the tub until it melted completely. She turned the water off when the bath was finished, and walked inside. She shivered as her body was wrapped in hot water. Dipping her head for a moment under the surface, she allowed the water to reach each inch of her being. The steaming water combined with the salt's gentle fragrance was very soothing, just what it wanted after the pressure to which it permitted itself to be taken during a scene.

She wasn't sure how long it had been, but it had been a while since the water had gone from cold and hot to dry. She was shocked by his presence above her; she jumped, and let out again a little yelp.

"SSHHHH" held up his finger to his lips, "It's me alone." He rushed in to check on her. She was reportedly in there for an hour and a half. He was still wearing the blanket, and sitting on the edge of the pool instead.

"Kneel over there facing the wall," he directed.

She turned toward the building, then stood on her knees. He got the ice bucket and filled it with water, put his fingers under her nose and poured the water over her head. He then took the water and had her hair lathered. In her half-asleep mind, she sat there, loving the sensation of her fingertips in her hair. For several minutes he'd massaged the shampoo into her scalp. With the fun of it she heard herself softly moaning.

Then, he held the hair lather over her back and

shoulders. For several minutes he massaged them, whispering in her ear how he loved having such a sweet little slut to play with as he traced the patterns of her welts from the cane and whips earlier during the scene there.

As he got out of the shampoo's lather he picked up the soap bar and went back down to her bottom. He mapped all the welts and scratches and massaged them there too, whispering to her to lean forward against the wall. She did comply. The cold tile felt terrific against her cheek and her soft flushing breasts.

She then felt his hands as he entered her on both sides of hers. His hard dick lay in the crack of her butt as he wrapped her body in a tight embrace. He started grinding it gently against her back as he kissed her neck and muttered to her shoulders what a good girl she was tonight, and what a pleasure she had given him in her submission. She found herself rubbing back into him, moaning a bit louder as the soap made between the two bodies a good lubricant. He began massaging her breasts and maulling them as he proceeded to rub into her leg. She could feel her belly and vagina start burning as her moans kept getting louder and louder.

Then, with a laugh, he whispered in her ear "SSSHHHHH, you're going to wake our neighbors," then kissed her and sat back on the edge of the pool.

He managed to wash her legs up until he hit the bath. He then took the ice bucket, filled it over and over again and rinsed all the soap out of her hair and back.

He instructed her to "turn around."

He pulled his knees close, as she stood up to turn, and this time forced her to kneel around him, leaving her wide open. In this place she complied with a blush feeling slightly insecure. He also took the soap, and started washing her front face. She stared at his paws as he mauled her breasts once more. He immediately went down and massaged the soap onto her uterus. When he made his way lower and lower, she could feel her body shivering.

He finally reached her cunt, and at first contact her entire body was shaking violently. He smiled, then began to rub her pussy lips outside. He massaged and massaged them until a little bit she started moaning and thrusting against his side.

"Hungry little bitch," he muttered while sliding a few fingers between her lips. He bent down at the same time and brought her nipple into his mouth.

She muttered shiveringly, "We shouldn't do this Dad. We can't stop." "Relax. "Whispered he. "Just enjoy the delights, bitch. I'll know when to stop. "When licking and scraping her breasts he rubbed his fingertips up and down on both sides of her clit. Her moans rose in intensity and she raised her pussy higher on his thighs closer to his dick. He was easy to slip his fingers from the top of her pussy lips all the way inside her. Her breathing was rapid, and her orgasm was getting close.

She began crying out between her moans "Oh God, Oh God."

"You can" was all he had to say and her entire body shuddered as her pussy clamped and pulsed around his fingertips as she let out a loud "OH GOD OH GOD OH GOD SIR!" And she buried her face biting and sucking into her throat, while her orgasm began to pulsate across her entire body.

He took up the ice bucket when she was done, and rinsed out her forehead. He told her to stand up after he rinsed her off, then stood up himself, picked up a towel and wrapped it around her. She kissed his cheek "Thank you Sir." She was still a little dizzy from her climax but it felt so good to have him taking such care of her after she gave her entire body to him for whatever discomfort or enjoyment he wanted to inflict on her at the club earlier.

He always felt of herself as a "daddy."

He opened the drain and blew the candles out, then left them.

Once she entered her bed, the room was pitch black. He led her to her room, sat down, washed off her body and hair and removing her towel. Her eyes in the dark had problems coping. She placed the towel on her pillow when he was done so she could smell the delicious rose aroma through the night and then climbed back into bed.

She lies on her side, wide-awake, with her back to his pillow. She listened to him get in his bed in the darkness of the house. Hundreds of emotions rattled in her head. Pictures of their scene from the beginning of the night, pictures of him touching her in the different ways he worked, pictures of her bath and the love his hands used to wash her, how his hand felt as he moved his fingertips across her clit and into her cunt. It was just too much. She laid there hoping, no, begging with the silence he was going to join her in bed. She had done that a long time before, with somebody else. Last night, her prayers went unanswered, and this night she was sure would be the same, any second she would hear his bed creak.

I even told herself that anyway he's off limits to me.

Just as she allowed herself to doze off she felt her

bed's covers lifting up against her back and his warm face. He had never left her bedside at all. He was nude, and was very hot in his head. He wrapped his arms around her back and pushed his rock hard cock between her legs.

"I couldn't sleep, always," he said.

"Neither could I, Sir," she muttered still in shock.

She couldn't believe it actually existed. She couldn't believe this thing she so badly wanted, had been waiting for the darkness was finally here.

Slowly rocking back and forth against her ass, he began to slide his dick in and out of her thighs while kissing her neck back. She lay there just shivering with desire.

Stop Oh my God! She so badly wanted to. She could sense the need burning deep inside her belly. Her cunt felt cold and she realized that it had been soaking wet. She still slid her finger down, just to test. Sure, she was dirty, and her legs were streaming out.

He kept pushing against her, slipping his dick in and out of her buttocks, starting to move a little upwards.

Stop Oh my God! She said to herself, I've got to stop him, we can't do this because she realized she was spreading her legs just a little bit more, encouraging her dick to be closer to her vagina.

Then she turned, and started to hug him. Each time he moved his dick through her thighs and it also bounced from the outside across to her pussy lips. She began whimpering just a little as they kissed, she had to resist, this was out of all their limits, but as he kept pumping his between her thighs she gradually found herself opening them up for him. She pushed back into his cock and deepened each of its thrusts.

She felt the tip of his cock disappear inside her after a couple of minutes of kissing and thrusting. Immediately, she pulled back and pressed her legs together. She whispered to him, "Sir, this is not something we should be doing. It's beyond both of our boundaries." "Tonight it's going to be okay, "he whispered back as he ground his dick again between her sopping wet legs. She was so soaked there was no "No Sir, we shouldn't" opposition, she whispered again. He bent in and started to kiss her a long, deep kiss, thrusting his cock a little further between his thighs.

"We should. Yea. You just as desperately want to. Look at you, all dirty. I've never seen a girl who's more happy to be fucked than you are now, "he answered.

With him on top, he rolled her up on her back and spread her legs wide open keeping his hands, his cock floating over her cunt. She heard his smile although she couldn't see him. She reached out for his cock and started to massage it.

 "Yeah, sir, you're right, I want it, I want it to be too fucking bad, so I can't do it, sir," she muttered to him, "but yes, I can do it." "I can let you listen to me, Sir, I can let you hear me writing beneath you, against you as I fuck my own hands and pet." She let go of his cock and gave him a taste of what she was thinking about, rolling her ass on his thighs while she played with both hands on her clit and cunt. She heard a low little groan coming over her from his mouth. He knew she was right, this was still tolerated and he just wanted to stay within his own limits that he had established in a small way.

Instead he leaned down, and began to lick and suck her nipples. "Tell me what a whore you are, play with that clit of yours." She reached up beneath her pillow; previously, she quietly hid a vibrator when he was in the tub showering. She took it and slid it deep inside her cunt, while her fingertips slid in small little circles around her clit. She started off smaller; with the vibrator, quick strokes, keeping time on her clit with her other hand, moving it in and out of.

"Sir, stroke your dick, can you stroke it on top of me, can you?" She was telling him.

She could feel him pulling above her on his cock; he even thrust his legs a little. She quickly swayed and writhed against his buttocks, her cunt gripping against the thrusting vibrator. He threw himself back against her, dick in his mouth, rubbing his fingertips along her side as he stroked over her. When he climaxed she could hear a man's familiar sound.

She started softly moaning, this was it, and now she was going to have her orgasm. Last time, she hadn't considered asking for permission.

"They're going to cum right now, aren't they? "He was gasping.

"Oh yes, Sir," she moaned softly "right now" and then, angrily. When her cunt clutched and pulsed upon her vibrator, she clutched his hands with hers.

"Keep on stroking, don't interrupt," he told her. She began to massage her pulsing cunt and clit, orgasm. Now he works his cock hard, thrusting between his fingers fast and furious. She continued writhing and now her moans were beginning to sound more like tears.

"Keep it up, slut on," he told her again.

She tried to keep stroking her clit, but the fire in her belly was always stoked by stroke and she couldn't even hold the pace.

"I can't Sir anymore," she screamed at him as she clenched her legs around him, squeezed her fingertips and lifted her pussy just under his stroking hand and pushed hard against it.

"MMMMMMMMMMMMMMMMMMMMMM Sir, I want to feel it, I want to taste your cock Captain! Let me feel your cock Yes, yes! "She begged him with each of her strokes as she pressed him against him. "Please Fuck me. Please. "Her entire body was on fire and she didn't care about any laws or boundaries, all she knew was that she never wanted to lose this flame. It would have been easy to rape her if he wished to do so.

Eventually, as her knuckles were running up and down with each stroke across her pussy lips, she heard him gushing and groaning as she felt his hot come splattering over her chest.

"MMMM, yeah, that's Sir, dump on me all that cum," she cooled at him, easing her hips back down on the bed. He just knelt between her thighs and felt her cum rubbing onto her stomach until it was all warm again.

She sat up when she was done, straddled his knees leaning on his dick over her open, wet cunt, and gave him a deep kiss.

"Thank you Sir" she said as she kissed him in his ear.

He muttered "thank you" as he got up and climbed into his bunk.

She laid there for a second before throwing back into a deep sleep.

Your Sexy Smile

I work full-time. I have been a bus driver for many years. This year, I happen to be driving for your children. Every morning, you and your children stand at the bus stop Every morning, you smile at me and flirt a little. In the afternoon, I bring your children to your house. You are my last stop of the day. I spend my evenings thinking about your sexy smile and fantasizing about all the wonderful things you could do to my body. The last day of school, you finally have the courage to ask me out. I agree to meet you at your house later that night. The plan is to go out and have a few drinks.

I'll come over to your house in a long flowing dress with red floral print. It's got a slit that goes all the way up to my hip. Spaghetti straps and a low neckline that shows off my cleavage beautifully. I combined it with strappy red block heels. The straps wrap my leg. When you open the door, look at me from top to bottom and lick your lips. My smile grows knowing that you like what you see. You compliment me and we go for a drink.

We'll talk for hours and enjoy each other's company.

You tell me you're a single father of three wonderful children. That you've been single for over a year, doing everything alone. You tell me that it is lonely and how much you miss the company of a good woman. You also tell me what you want from a woman, but I notice that you are holding something back. I'm telling you that I'm a single parent too.

I have two children, and I've been doing this all by myself for six years. I also mention that I haven't had sex in over a year. You ask me why, and tell me I'm a beautiful woman and should have no problem finding a man. I smile at your compliment and drop my eyes. I feel the heat on my cheeks as I debate telling you my secret. You reach out your hand and stroke my cheek with your right index finger. The night has gone so well, and I'm afraid to ruin it.

I take a deep breath and decide that the best way to do it is to just do it, like ripping off a Band-Aid. I look up and tell you that I haven't been with a man in over a year because I am a submissive person who needs a dominant man. A master man who dominates her sexually, but allows her control over her own life when she is in the midst of the norms. I tell you, I need a man who can use me as his personal, dirty little slut, but who is still a good master who treats me right. You almost smile, then your face becomes solemn when you ask me if I am ready to prove it.

I look down at my hands and think about it. After a moment I look up and ask you to kiss me so that I can make up my mind. You get up and lean over the table. You take my face in your hands and whisper to me that nothing would make you happier. You kiss me long and hard. You explore my mouth with your tongue and leave me breathless when you pull away. A moment later I can still feel you on my lips and feel a burst of energy reaching my innermost being. I look into your eyes and tell you: "Yes, I am ready to prove it. You only live once, right?

I look down at my hands to think about your challenge. After a moment I look up to ask you to kiss me, but you get up and wave me to silence. "A true submissive does not make demands unless he begs," you reply flatly. When you come around the table to my seat, lean down after you have collected the hairs on the back of my head. You hold me firmly but gently with your lips, which are only a few centimetres from mine, and shout,

"Do you understand?

My eyes are wide open as our conversation turns to my darkest desires, and I manage to stammer "Yes, yes".

"Good girl." Her hand lets go of my hair as the other hand cupping my face: "Nothing would make me happier than your surrender. You growl softly before you take my mouth and kiss me long and hard. Your tongue explores my mouth, gets entangled with mine and leaves me breathless. As you pull away, the hard glint shimmers in your eyes as I lift trembling fingers to my lips. A moment later I can still feel you on my lips and a surge of energy shocks through my core.

I meet your eyes with mine. "Yes. I will prove it to you." And risk it. "Master."

You instruct me to go back to my house, put on something slutty and take you home in thirty minutes on my bus. Thirty minutes later I arrive at your house on my bus as ordered, wearing the same red strappy heels and a naughty schoolgirl outfit. I think it's appropriate, since you asked me to drive the bus. The top is black and see-through. It has short sleeves and a deep V-neck. It's also a low-cut top. My stomach is almost completely naked. I have decided not to wear a bra, but a tie that goes with my skirt instead. My tie is a little longer than the shirt itself. The skirt is red plaid with black lace trimming and rests nicely on the middle of my ass cheeks. In the front it is a bit longer, just long enough that you can't see my panties when I stand up. Not that the panties I've chosen for tonight have much to hide. Tonight, I'm wearing a red thong with black trimming.

I feel slutty and exposed and I love every second of it. When I get to your house, I notice you standing outside with your own backpack. I smile and open the door. You drink in my appearance as you get on the bus. You sit in the first row of seats, but on the opposite side to me. You tell me that I have done a good job to be on time and I smile. You instruct me to drive to a dirt road a few miles away. I turn onto a heavily wooded road, and about two miles later you let me stop and park the bus.

You tell me to show you my submissive position. I get

out of my seat and kneel beside it. I spread my legs wide, fold my arms behind my back and look down at the floor in front of me. You tell me: "Good girl, then ask me if I have hard boundaries and a chosen safe word.

"Sir, anal. Feces and water sports. Drifting. I can't stand people fiddling with my feet, sir. What happens between us must remain private. I am a trustworthy member of the community; I work with people's children, and it would not be good for me if anyone found out about me. Your head tends to bend speculatively when you ask if that's all there is to it.

I say, "Um, sir, there are two things. Sir, I don't do ass to mouth resuscitation, and I don't want to have bruises or welts like they would if you hit me with a stick. I don't have a problem with whipping and flogging and whatnot, except for the bruises. Sir."

You cross your arms while your eyes get hard and sarcastically ask me if there is something I actually agree with. My cheeks blossom with your displeasure as you ask me again, "Is that all?" I nod my head, "Yes.

Your anger increases and you grab my hair and pull my head back. With the other hand you roughly grab my jaw and tell me: "I can't hear your head rattling from there. From now on I expect you to answer me with your words.

If I answer quickly, I say, "Yes, sir. I'm sorry, master." You let go of me and tell me to take up my position again and answer your question. I say, "Yes, sir, that's all."

"Oh? No safe word?" My face turns crimson again. "Yellow," I murmured.

"Hmm. Appropriate."

You walk away from me towards the back of the bus. I can tell you're processing everything I told you. I'm taking the moment to examine you. I look at your ass and the way you walk. I love your build and the way you carry yourself. When you reach the back of the bus, turn around and look at me. You catch me looking at you like this.

"Tsk, tsk, tsk, tsk. You must be very rusty or a very bad submissive. A good submissive knows that making eye contact without being addressed is bad etiquette. Bad girl. Cost you two lashes."

I apologize and look at the floor.

As soon as you arrive at the front of the bus, open the doors and let me up. You leave the bus and stand outside. You grab every door and look up at me and instruct me to lie down over the driver's seat, facing the back of the bus, and tell me that you want to see my ass. You tell me to put my hands behind my back. I do what I'm told quickly.

Once I'm in position, you walk back up the stairs. I feel your eyes all over my ass, and it's making my pussy tingle. I know now that if you looked, you could see that my cunt is wet. My cheeks turn pink when I think of what I must look like in this position. I can hear you taking a deep breath. A short moment later I feel your hands graze my ass while you fold my skirt onto your back.

You caress it and my thighs. I moan softly. It's been so long since anyone has touched me. You sit on your knees and inspect me. You pull my ass cheeks apart and watch the string of my panties sink deeper into the crevice.

You kiss each butt cheek and hook your finger under the string of my panties and slowly slide it up and down under the string as you start talking. You tell me that anal intercourse is the only one of my boundaries that you don't want to break. It doesn't have to be tonight, but if we go any further, it will be a requirement at some point. This is the moment when I put your finger on my

wrinkled hole. It ripples under your touch and I take a sharp breath while you say, "Relax. It's a nice, tight, little hole, and I can't wait to use it."

I am relaxing. You slide your finger down a little further and push that little piece of cloth aside. You get a full view of my wet pussy. Your mouth curves into a smile. "You must be a submissive little bitch. I've barely touched you and I can see the moisture coming out of your pink little pussy. I'm getting red again. I can hear you inhaling my scent, and my blush turns bright red. Your finger's running across my slit as you keep talking.

You're telling me you're not gonna push my limits tonight. Tonight you're gonna tie me up and use me, and if I prove to be a good bitch for you, then we can talk about our relationship between Dom and Sub.

I'm nodding eagerly. "Yes, sir."

You're going to stand up again and pat me on the right ass cheek. I jump a little bit because I wasn't expecting it. They rub it roughly and grab my ass cheek and squeeze it hard. It stings just enough to let me know that you left a red handprint. You pull your hand back and admire your work. "Very nice. You'll do well." Then you ask me if I'm ready for my punishment of two fisticuffs earlier.

Swallowing, I manage to stammer, "Y-yes, M-master." How quickly I am on the verge of tears.

"Good. Count out every sway out loud. If I don't hear you count out loud and clear, we start again. Do you understand?"

"Yes, sir."

-

The first blow hits me hard on the left cheek. I won't jump this time, but I'll say "shit" as soon as you connect. I take a deep breath and say "one". You shake your head and tell me, "I'm disappointed in your little submarine. A real submarine should know how to count right." You tell me to say the number, and sir, and then a thank you for punishing you as you deserve. I apologize to you and I'm mentally preparing for my next assignment.

You gently rub my ass cheek and ask me, "Are you ready to be a good bitch and try again? I answer, "Yes, sir." The next blow feels harder than the last as it lands on my right cheek and brings tears to my eyes. I take a short breath and say, "One, sir. Thank you for teaching me, sir. May I have another, please, sir?" You like that very much. You fondle both my ass cheeks and give the right one a tender kiss. I give a sigh while you comfort me.

They tell me that the next blow will be the hardest yet and ask me if I understand. I say softly, "Yes, sir." Your hand immediately touches my pussy. I scream in pain and tears come down on my face. It takes me a few moments to get my composure back. Softly I say, "Two, sir. Thank you for teaching me, sir. May I have another, please?" You kneel beside me, rubbing my aching pussy and telling me that I did well and that you're proud of me. You say that two lashes was the punishment I deserved and that I won't get another now.

You turn me over and you kiss me hard. You tell me to turn on the interior lights in the back of the bus and go to the sixth seat on the bus. I push myself up from the seat, turn on the lights, then get up and go where you directed me. You sit on your seat and rummage around in your bag. You find what you are looking for and approach me with a ball gag, leg irons and handcuffs. You tell me to stand with my feet together and turn towards you. You put the handcuffs on my ankles, but don't hook them together.

You bring your hands up against my body from my ankles and make me tremble. You tell me to open wide and you push the ball in my mouth and turn me around so that you can fasten it on the back. You tell me to turn around and face you. I do as I am told, another delicious tremor runs through me. You tell me to strip and keep my tie and panties on. I slowly take my shirt off over my head and feel my tits burst open. My nipples harden immediately. I lower my skirt down to my ankles and step out of it.

I begin to reach for my heels and you stop me and tell me to keep them on. You put my hands behind my back and caress my chest at the same time. Then you lick each nipple, one by one, and then you suck hard on them so that they make a popping sound when they slip out of your mouth. They stand up and tell me to turn around and look to the back of the bus. Then you pull my hands behind me and put the other handcuffs on my wrists. This makes my chest stick out. They tell me to stay facing the back of the bus and put one knee on each seat.

My legs are openly spread across the aisle of the bus.

They reach down and tie each of my ankles with the small ring on the ankle cuffs and a tie from your pocket to the bars that are under the seat. You stand behind me and press your body against my bound back arms. You grip your hands around me and start squeezing my tits. You pull on my nipples while you bite and kiss my neck and collarbone.

You keep pulling and rolling on my nipples until they hurt from your abuse. You pull them out as far as you can stretch them, and then you do the same by pulling them up and down. You seem happy with my tolerance for it and the distance you can stretch them. I have drool running down my chin and dripping on my chest. You are smearing it on my chest while you are telling me: "You might be a good little slut I could use after all.

You stick around, keep playing with my tits with one hand and slide your other hand down my stomach to my panties. I can feel you sticking a finger in my waistband and pushing it right and left, back and forth. You growl in my ear that you fuck this sperm-loving pussy and that I'm going to love being your dirty sperm slut tonight.

Your finger slides further down until you reach my clitoris. You snap your finger and slide it further down my slit. In the opposite direction you take your hand out of my panties and rub my juices under my nose and on my upper lip. You tell me to pick it up and smell it. Then you suck on your fine one and tell me, "You taste wonderful... ...for a little sperm bitch." Without warning, you get down on your knees and slide my panties aside.

You look at my pussy and tell me I'm a dripping mess. My pussy lips are a bit swollen from my previous punishment, but you like the way it looks and smells. You tell me you can't wait to use my little pink pussy any way you want. Then you pull your tongue with a slow lick from front to back over my swollen pussy. I moan and let my head fall to my chest. I stick my ass out a little more.

You tell me that I have a very good pussy for a dirty sperm bitch, and you wonder how tight it is. You're talking more to yourself at this point than to me. I'm whimpering with anticipation. You take both hands, you pull up my pussy lips and tell me it's such a nice pink pussy. I try to thank you, but with the gag in my mouth it comes out all distorted and in the end I let a stream of drool run down my chest.

You slap my ass and say, "Shut up, bitch." I bow down in devotion. You rub my ass for a second and say, "That's more like it." You spread my pussy lips again and stick your tongue in it, fuck me with it for a few moments with your tongue. I roll around on your face. You stick a finger in and tell me to shut up, or you can untie me right now and we'll be done in a second.

I'll stand still like a statue and try to say "yes, sir" one more time. I got drool in my panties. You keep on fucking me with one finger, then with two fingers. If I take the third finger with ease, you ask me how much I think I can take. I try to answer, but it's all just a mumble You ask me what that was while you're driving your fingers faster and harder and faster into my pussy

I am panting violently through wildly flared nostrils at this point. You're telling me I don't have permission to cum. You're not done with me. That I'd better not jerk off when I know what's best for me. Then you insert your fourth finger. I feel the warm feeling deep in my stomach. It tells me that I'm going to cum hard and it's going to be a gush.

I start to shake my head, no, and scream "I'm coming!" into the ball gag. They do a few more hits, then quickly pull the hand away. You wipe my juices on my thigh, and I cry about your fingers not being in my pussy anymore. You giggle and call me a needy little bitch. I'm whimpering again because I didn't come to jerk off. I'm also very proud of myself for not coming and doing what I was told. They tell me I'm a good little whore and that I'm being rewarded for it.

They loosen my ball gag and remove it. You slide under me and come towards me. When I look at myself from top to bottom, I see in your expression that I am a wreck and I know it. I blush violently as your eyes wander over my body. My make-up has run over my face in streaks. I have red lines from the ball gag straps on my cheeks. I drool down to my panties. My nipples are so hard and painful after your touch. Between the drool and my juices my panties are soaked to see how wet they are. I know that when I look down, I see a puddle under me.

They lift up my chin to look into my eyes. A pinch on my nipple confirms that you tell me I look like a beautiful sperm slut. You order me to tell you if I have come. You're sure I didn't, but you want to hear it from me. Your fingers squeeze my nipple a little harder, pulling hard on it. If I tell you, "No, sir, that whore didn't come. This one was a good bitch and did what was asked of her," you let go of my nipple and pat me on the tit.

I scream and you tell me, "Yes or no, come on, bitch!"

"Yes, sir! I'm sorry, sir! Fresh tears streaming down my cheeks.

You tell me you're gonna fuck my pussy, then you fuck my mouth. And only after I clean your cock will I get your permission to cum.

I nod my head and immediately try to correct myself by saying "Yes, sir". But I'm not fast enough. You frown, but tell me it's okay that I fucked up. That I tried to correct my mistake, but I'm still being punished for it. I sigh and look down and say, "Yes, sir. I'm sorry, sir."

They tell me that this time I'm going to get four punches, and I'd better count them right, or it's going to get a lot worse for me. This time I say, "Yes, sir."

I keep watching your face as you rub your hands together, which creates friction and warms your hands. Then you slap me on both titties, hard and at the same time. I yell, "One, sir! Thank you for teaching me, sir! May I have another, please?" between sobs. They smile quite cruelly and say, "Yes, you may, bitch. You've earned it."

You rub your hands together again, and this time the punches are going to my areolas. The sting makes my nipples stand upright and burn in pain. I sob harder. After a moment I pull myself together and repeat my mantra "Thank you". They smile again and tell me that maybe I will have another one. I pull myself together as you rub your hands together again and this time one hand comes down hard on my left tit and grabs my nipple. I scream, "Fuck! Ooooohhh, fuck!" and take a deep breath and repeat, "T-thank you, s-sir. M-may I have another one, please?" My voice raises in a crescendo of pain. You smile and quickly come down on the other tit. You catch my other nipple, like you did with the last punch.

There are tears in my eyes all the time now, and I take a few deep breaths before thanking you one last time. I open my mouth to ask for one more, and you shut me up. I slide back under my legs, get up and stand behind me. I hear your zipper open and your pants fall to the floor. You kick off your shoes and step out of your pants and then kick them behind you.

I feel you aligning your cock with my pussy and rubbing your head against it a couple of times. You remind me not to cum. You spread my pussy lips open and push your cock in a jerk all the way into my soaked but narrow channel. My breath stops. Your cock is big and thick and I feel it being stretched mercilessly by him. You pull it all the way out, slap my ass and tell me to be quiet.

My pussy's dripping wet and your cock's missing. You bend down and lick my pussy. You untie my ankles and tell me, "On your knees, look at my face, bitch." I do as I'm told. I turn around and I kneel down in front of you. You stroke your dick with your hand, then you tell me to open it wide and suck it like a good bitch. I open my mouth and take about a third of your cock between my lips and over my tongue. I pull it back, stick out my tongue and start licking it all over. You put your hand on the back of my head and tell me to suck it while you press my head on your cock.

You keep your hand on the back of my head but give me back control as I lead you deeper and deeper with every stroke. Tell me what a good cocksucker mouth I have and how well I do my job. You tell me that you want to hear me gagging on your cock and that you want me to look you in the eyes while you do it. I mumble "Y-ll-esss, Sthirr" with your dick in my mouth. I look you right in the eyes and I swallow your cock until I gag. I see your eyes roll back into your head while I choke on your shaft.

I do it again. This time you grab my head with both hands and hold my head still while you fuck my mouth. You're fucking him harder and faster with every stroke. I choke so often that my throat burns. Fresh tears are streaming down my face. You tell me you're gonna cum and I'm supposed to show you before I swallow. You squeeze my mouth one last time, hold me on your cock while I wave my hands behind me with my cuffed hands. The bulbous head blocking my throat swells up, rippling pulses run down my flattened tongue while your sperm squirts out in many hot bubbles.

One of them hits the back of my throat. One hits my chin when I pulled back too far trying to breathe. The last one lands right on my tongue. You put your hands on the seats near you to calm yourself down while you look down at me. I tilt my head back, on my knees, tongue out, mouth wide open, and show you your sperm. You tell me what a dirty sperm slut I am and that you enjoyed using me tonight and that I can swallow. I swallow your sperm and thank you for doing it and for using me.

You tell me that I have been a good girl and that it is time for me to get my reward. You let me sit back in the seat and stretch my feet in the air. I put them on the seats on either side of me. I'll spread them out for you. You get down on your knees and press your face into my needy pussy. Your lips go straight to my lust bud and suck it hard while your tongue swirls it and licks it mercilessly. Your fingers find my soaking wet opening, rush in to fuck me to the point where I go crazy with my desperate desire. You get up and pause.

Beg me to come, my pretty, dirty sperm slut," you demand.

"Please, sir," I say, "C-can I come?

"No," your terse answer comes. "Not before I hear you begging. Really begging."

"Please, sir, may your sperm slut come? I-I-I'm so close it hurts. I want to cum. I need to jerk off! P-please, sir? Please, sir? Master?"

"No, not yet, bitch." Your last denial is a cruel grin.

"Please, please, please, please, please, please, please, please, please, sir," I sing desperately. "PLEASE!! Uunnghh..." my summoned plea ends in a grunt as you press four fingers into me until your thumb stops your thrust. I pant violently: "P-please. C-can. I.

Sperm?"

"You may cum, bitch. All over my face." When your mouth comes back to my pussy, I'm gushing all over your face. You swallow it greedily as you continue to finger me. You also suck on my clit and delay my orgasm as long as possible. I scream and cry and laugh and finally writhe in lustful pain while the sensations overwhelm me. My thighs cling to your head while I try to stop your onslaught.

"N-no...n-nothing more. I can't go on. I can't go on... Lord. Please..." I beg weakly, this time I beg for a break.

You raise your head and look at me, and there's... recognition in your eyes. Your smile illuminates them, and my own gratitude skyrockets when I hear your last two words.

"Good girl."

A Bisexual Subject

A rolling romp of hardcore menagerie. You'll find everything except plain old vanilla sex. For those women who like to see the boys, or who prefer to see the girls, the Berlin strings are actually just two of my most treasured memories in my personal journey of sexual discovery as a young adult. The rest is, well, some truth, some fiction, some fantasy.

Even though it's written to a bisexual subject, that's not exactly what this story is actually about. It's all about throwing society's irrationally restrictive prejudices and phobias, and assessing the defined masculine and feminine roles in the bedroom doorway. If it is possible to put aside jealousy, be accepting and discuss fantasies with your spouse, the outcomes could be really rewarding.

"So you want to play with the boys, huh,?" she states as she awakens my buttocks. "Tell me all the dirty little things you did, you naughty boy."

I have my hands on her pussy, slipping my finger

between her lips. I believe back at an all-boy romp in a hotel in Berlin, Germany. "You actually want me to inform you of all the naughty things your filthy little husband did?"

"Tell me what infant, and do not leave out anything cause I will know whether you're lying or not!" she yelled as she gives my cock a hard squeeze.

Talking dirty makes her sexy. Plus it gets me hot, too.

"We're on leave in Berlin. We've been out dancing and partying in the discos. The four people returned to their hotel area. We're all wound up and sexy from each dirty dancing and from all the sexual innuendos, and we wind up paired off to bed. My friend is lying back, and now I'm kneeling between his thighs. I feel naughty and lively. His hard little penis is pointing upwards, and now I have to take care of it.

"It goes all the way into my mouth, into the back of my neck. I've never done this before. It's my first time giving another man head. I toy him for a while, carrying him from my mouth and my lips running up and down the bottom of his shaft, then engulf his prick in one quick motion.

Suck, suck, and treating him like this is wicked. I bob up and down on his penis as his breath comes out in short pants, in rhythm with my strokes. He's within my hands and I really like it. I grasp his buttocks as he thrusts in my mouth. His hands are on my head, along with his fingers clenching my own hair.

"With the pace quickening, I feel him getting close. He pushes against me, suggesting me he's about to cum, but I shake my head and keep moving. His thighs quiver and he lets out a lengthy 'ahhhhhhh' because he cums.

"The bottom of his penis pulses against my tongue as his hot cum shoots the roof of the mouth. I maintain my mouth over him, milking him until he's spent, then disrobe him and sit. Meeting his eyes with a glowing grin, I lick my lips, then lean my head and swallow, blowing his mind. He reaches up and brings me to him until we're pressed closely together. Kissing me, his tongue probes deep into my mouth, tasting himself in my breath."

Her hips are rocking back and forth against my palms as I slip them in and out of her pussy. "Come on baby, tell me, I wish to hear more," she moans as she strokes my shaft. She's lying down with her eyes shut, painting the images in her mind.

"I'm back in Berlin alone, and also another older guy seduces me in a bar. He's in his thirties and I'm only twenty. An American like me, he is likely in the army. He won't tell me his name, but he also doesn't wish to know mine. He just wishes to spend the night together.

"We go into my hotel room, and he chooses me, then undresses me while caressing me. I'm trembling like a virgin, and for this particular night, I really am.

"We're lying on our hands on the bed like a spoon and he is behind me. He's stroking me, which makes him breathe into my ear. He puts on a condom and lubes me, getting me prepared with his finger. I'm trembling as he puts the head of his cock to my ass. I'm concerned about what he would believe.

"I look back at him and he reassures me with a grin. He is bigger and more powerful than I am and he will bring me pain or pleasure in his whim. But he is gentle and I trust him. He enters me slowly but insistently, and there is nothing that I can do to stop him. I believe this has to be what it is like for a girl to be penetrated, to give yourself up entirely."

"Come on me baby, come upon me. Stroke while you inform me of your story." I straddle her torso and wrap my hands around my engorged erection. She lubes her hands and dominates me. "Come on baby, let me that the rest of your story" She chooses the head of my prick into her mouth, then circles her tongue on the tip.

"He is very seasoned and knows exactly what he's doing. He moves gradually, getting used to sense inside me. The atmosphere is intense. On the border, that lean boundary between pain and pleasure. The longer I relax, the better it gets. And he's so great. I'm so fucking hard, harder than I have ever been in my entire life. Every thrust he makes appears to pump me up much more. I'm a bundle of nerve endings, concentrating on each feeling.

The rest of the production has dropped off, and that is my whole world. His hot pole of the flesh is absorbed by my intestines. Probing and throbbing, a lifetime of pleasure. I'm stroking myself and stoking my passion. His thumping and pulsing are escalating up us, to the summit of this precipice. Hard muscles and perspiration, grinding and thrashing and crying, then a blind explosion. My white sexy cum is wrapped in air, suspended by the strobe of my brain. We come back collectively, landing flat on our backs in post-orgasmic bliss."

"Cum for me baby, cum in my mouth. I need to taste you." She's never done that before, and it's the first time anybody has done this for me. I look down at her and into her eyes. She is honest, wanting to please.

"You actually need me to cum in your mouth?"

"Yes baby, yes. Come on, give it to me." She's working her finger into my bum as I pound on my shaft. Her mouth is near the head of my penis, sucking me and licking me with her tongue.

"Oh fuck, fuuckkk!"

I make a white ribbon across her mouth. She takes me in, then out, and yet another dab on her cheek. She squeezes her lips on the tip, then takes me straight back into her mouth, stroking me with her lips because my spasms subside.

I lean down and hold her head in my own hands. A glorious mess. I kiss her, my tongue inside her mouth, then her tongue in mine, sharing my cum.

"You're such a naughty girl," I state as I wipe her face off with a towel. "And I love you a lot." I work my way down her body, licking and kissing as I move. "Tell me everything you do, as soon as your husband is not around. Tell me the way you play on your own. Tell me all the naughty things you do."

"I've been dozing and wait until the children have gone to college and you've left. Perhaps a sexy fantasy, which makes me wet and aroused. I get the jar of lube and my vibrator. I'm sure that the door is closed and turn on some songs. Occasionally I wear a picture, a naughty bi-sex one. I see the boys suck each other and fuck one another and make each other cum."

"Oh, indeed? You want to watch the boys play with one another. Does it make you hot?"

"Oh, it gets me quite hot. I lift my breasts and lick my nipples, and then I make them hard. I circle my nipples with the vibrator, then pour lube into my pussy. It gets me so wet and tingly as I stroke my vibrator over my clit and in my pussy. I lie and rock my hips into the vibrator as I lightly caress my clit.

"It seems really great and the film is making me horny. I could cum straight away. However, I would like it to continue, so I quit that for a bit and watch the film. The vibrator is filling me and keeping me on the border. I see them take their hot cum, and now I'm dying to cum, but I return, not daring to proceed.

"From what the next scene is based on, I move the vibrator ever so gradually. It's the one I've been waiting for, the one which makes me grit my teeth and curl my feet and tear out my hair.

"It's a spectacle with just two couples. They're kissing and sucking and licking all over each other. Among those girls is lying on her back, with a few of those guys taking long licks at her pussy. Her clit is tough and she yells every time his tongue slides.

"Another man kisses her neck and runs his hands over her entire body. Another woman is so gloomy, kneeling over and spreading herself to the camera, then fingers her clit. She sensuously kisses the girl, using their tongues to dance against one another. Licking her way to the lady's breast, she suckles her erect nipple, then teases the tip with her tongue."

"Do you also want to watch the women? I bet that makes you sexy if they lick each other's fairly pink pussys."

"Oh , I'm sooo sexy. I feign one of these is with me. The vibrator is in her hands, and my hands are her tongue."

"Oh really? You want to have the girls place their hands on your pussy." I lie down between her thighs and slip two fingers into her slippery snatch. "Is this what they do to you, baby? Can they do it in this way?"

"Oh, just like this."

"And you also enjoy when they lick at your hard little clitty. Can they lick it like this?" I lick my tongue along her clit, then tickle it with suggestion.

"Hello! Just, like this!"

"Tell me what else she does to you, baby. Tell me how it makes you feel."

"She chooses her hands from my pussy and slides her tongue between my pussy lips. She moves to me with her tongue and gently caresses my clit with her finger. Oh, that is so gloomy, with her tongue in me. My pussy's so succulent, making squishing sounds as she pushes in and out. I'm so hot and sexy. She knows exactly what to do."

Mirroring her voice, my tongue slides between her luscious labia. I am pussy drunk with her scent, and along with her forehead, is sweet velvet on my tongue. Her hard little nub pulsates with joy from my feathery fingertip. Impaling her with my tongue and suctioning out, I devor her gnawing cunt.

Intoxicated with lust, I proceed to rim myself around and down her bittersweet backdoor. The purpose of my tongue moves into her buttocks, penetrating her marginally.

"Oh, she is so horrible, sticking her tongue into me like this!" My nose was buried in her dripping pussy, and she's practically gushing, she's so moist. I'm unashamedly lathered and stung by ambrosia.

I must breathe and proceed to stimulate her clit with my mouth. My lips are glistening with her juices. I slip my fingers into her; two in front and one in rear. She rides my hands and face, gripping the back of my head with one hand. Reaching under her leg she catches my wrist with her other hand, pummeling my hands into her pussy and ass.

"Oh, make me cum!" She thrusts hard against my face. "That's it, you naughty girl!"

She clenches her muscles, tightening around my palms. Two rings of iron, buffered with her soft glossy sheaths. The strength of her orgasm is overpowering because I stroke her, wringing every last spasm from her flesh. Her capacity to sustain her discharge is wonderful.

A couple of ideas and phrases, and a little stimulation, built her to orgasm paramount. Obviously, that's what we do, once we use our dreams to fuel our climaxes. Doing this times is simply so much better.

The Favorite Club

She had him right where she wanted him.

Brianna had never felt so accomplished her whole life. And she was yet to get started with the plan she'd laid out, so there were more feelings of accomplishment where that came from. She had always known there was a way to beat a bully without using her fists, but could never have thought this would work with her beast of a husband. She'd been married to Sandler for three years. He hadn't been a beast from the start and has been nothing short of a Romeo. But she realized just now narcissistic the man truly was. All he cared about was himself. She had put up with all his bullshit for so long.

It was time to show him that roles could switch.

And there was no better day to get back at him than on a chilly Sunday morning. As usual, the man had returned home in a drunken mess. She knew without a doubt that he'd been to his favorite club and had probably wasted some hard-earned cash on a whore or two. His drunkenness has made it all too easy for her to strip him naked and restrain him to the bed. Now here she was, sitting at her dressing table with her eyes fixated on him. The man, motionless as a log, lay supine on their king-sized bed. His chest rose and fell as he breathed, but that was as far as his movements went.

Brianna glanced up at the wall clock. It was a few minutes past eight in the morning. She'd thought he would be up by now. She decided to give him a few more minutes to round up his sleep.

And then, just as though he'd read her thoughts, he stirred. She straightened her spine, a smile darting across her face.

"Wakey wakey," she said in a sing-song voice.

Sandler's eyes fluttered open. He groaned, his lips parting to let out a yawn. His hands twitched in an apparent attempt to cup his mouth, but they stayed fixed on the bed. His eyes widening with obvious confusion, he moved his hands again. This time, he tried to move his legs as well, but they didn't budge.

He stood no chance against the thick ropes she had restrained him with. The loops were strong enough to withstand his beastly tendencies, so when he started to growl and struggle, his hands and legs flailing on the bed as he tried to break free, so it didn't come as a surprise to Brianna. She would only be surprised if he didn't put up a show like this.

"You know," she said, "struggling like this will only cause the ropes to bite into your skin."

"Untie me," he ordered. "Or I swear I will—"

"Oh, darling, you will do nothing at all, believe me. If there's anyone who is in a position to give orders right now, it certainly isn't you." She rose from her chair, the six heels of her stiletto-heeled shoes perforating the transitory silence following her words.

Sandler was about to speak again, but at the sight of her, he could only gape. She was dressed in white thigh-high stockings and a garter belt, her breasts hiding in a lacy white bra. She found it intriguing how Sandler was clearly upset, but his body seemed to have a mind of its own. His cock leaped to life at the sight of her, preparing itself to push through her tight pussy.

"Hot, aren't I?" She winked at him.

She'd never dressed so sensually for him, so he probably never thought she had it in her. She advanced toward him, her hips swaying with each step. Locks of wavy blonde hair settled on her chest, hiding her cleavage.

She whipped her hair back, her eyes aglow with lust. "Sleep well, darling?"

She waited for a response, and when it didn't come, she chuckled. She didn't need his response anyway.

"I take that as a yes." She mounted the bed and started crawling between his legs. She leaned toward him, her breasts barely an inch away from his cock. She lowered her head some more, and then she breathed through her mouth, letting her steamy breath tickle his torso.

While she crawled her way toward his face, she could feel him trembling beneath her. And when his stomach clenched hard, she couldn't hold back a laugh. She dropped her ass, making a chair out of Sandler's torso.

Sandler groaned, his Adam's apple bobbing as he swallowed hard.

Brianna's lips found his left ear, and then she whispered, "There's a camera, Sandler."

Sandler bristled.

She laughed. "Dear husband, you see that, over there?"

Without turning around she pointed at an alarm clock on the dressing table. "That's a spy camera, darling."

"No!" Sandler shook his head, disbelieving.

Brianna chuckled. "Yes, darling."

Once again, Sandler tried to break free from the restraints, but his action yielded no results. It only had him rubbing against Brianna's pussy. She bit her lower lip to suppress a moan as his skin rubbed her through her crotchless panties. She could feel her pussy juice pooling beneath her. She glided back and forth, smearing Sandler's stomach with the natural lube.

"Now," she said, "here's what happens. You have to submit yourself to me, darling, and do whatever I request of you. Else, this video goes viral and everyone, including your silly little bitches, will see you tied up and powerless, while I humiliate you for the silly excuse of a man that you are."

"No you won't," he said.

"That's what you think?" She giggled. "You are so, so funny when you wanna be, Sandler. I mean, this is you trying to be funny, isn't it?"

She didn't wait for him to respond. "Has to be! I mean, you don't expect me to sign the divorce papers and walk away without giving you a memory to last a lifetime? Or do you?"

"What do you want, Brianna?"

Brianna grinned. She loved the tremor in his voice when he spoke with so much rage. She could almost see the fume escaping his ears.

"I wanna give you a memory to remember when we go our separate ways, Sandler," she said. "Please let me know if I have to say this again."

Sandler groaned.

Brianna slipped back again, and then forward, making his skin sleek with her juices. "You love it when I do this, huh? When I smear my pussy juice all over you like some high-end lotion?"

She glided back once again, bumping so hard into his cock that he jumped from the impact.

Sandler groaned harder. "Oh, God."

"There is no God, darling," she said. "Only you and I. Oh, and Sergio."

"Sergio?" he asked.

"Well, say hello." She reached back to grab his cock, and then she squeezed.

He let out a voiceless scream. She laughed, watching his dark mouth as his lips flew open. She didn't hear the door open or shut, but when Sandler gazed behind her with a horrified face, she knew they were not alone anymore.

Sergio was here.

"What did you think?" She made a face, feigning surprise. "That I was all dressed up for you?"

She clicked her tongue and shook her head, her lips stretching into a smile.

"No way, darling," she said. "I only entertain real men. Men like you with five-inch cocks deserve none of that. They're useful though, to clean me up after I've been fucked so bad. I wonder how I put up with you and your lack for so long. But I'm done now, because darling, I've had enough of your petite cock to last a lifetime."

She squeezed his cock again. From his clenching jaw, she could tell he was gritting his teeth, trying hard not to be vocal.

"What now?" she teased, letting go of his cock. "You won't cry anymore? Is it because of Sergio? Shy now, are..."

She trailed off as Sergio's palm found her back. His palm glided down toward her ass, and then he snaked his arm around her hips. She turned sideways to kiss him, an exaggerated moan escaping her when he squeezed her breasts. Sergio was stark naked, his huge cock ready to plunge deep inside her. She wrapped the fingers of her left hand around his shaft, gently stroking him while he kissed her.

She broke the kiss and nibbled her lower lip. "Oh fuck! Here's a real man. A real fucking man..."

She looked up into Sergio's baby blue eyes, a smile breaking out on her face as she found him grinning. They'd never met before, and she'd only found him on Tinder, but she'd seen from his nude photos that he had a monster between his legs.

"Mmh!" she hummed.

She licked her lips and turned toward Sandler who had suddenly turned speechless. With her left hand still wrapped around Sergio's cock, she pointed at it with her right index finger and gave it a rather vigorous shake.

"You see this right here?" she asked. "This is a real cock. I'd say it is eight inches..."

"Nine, actually," Sergio corrected. He buried his face in her neck and started to smother her with kisses.

She tilted her head sideways to accommodate his lips on her neck. "Nine fucking inches right here!"

She heaved a sigh as he unhooked her bra, and then she giggled as he buried his face between her breasts, flicking his tongue around them while he slipped his hand between her swollen pussy lips. Sergio rose to his feet and grabbed his cock, aiming it at her face like a gun. From where she sat, she could give him a blowjob without having to adjust her position. The thought of giving the endowed man a blowjob while she pinned Sandler down with her weight was too juicy not to entertain. She grabbed Sergio's cock once again. His girth pushed her fingers apart. He had apparently gotten thicker and longer in the few seconds she'd let go.

She brought her lips to his cock, and just as the thick head met her lower lip, she turned toward Sandler. "What now? You didn't actually think I was going to fuck you, did you?"

All smiles, she turned toward Sergio and took him in her mouth. He tore her lips apart and sank deep inside of her, past her teeth. She moved her head back and forth, setting the pace, even though his hand rested on her head. She soon picked up the pace, sucking him nice and fast. Spittle gathered in her mouth and sought to escape through the corners. She let them. They tickled down her mouth, spilled onto his cock, making her lips glide effortlessly.

His moaning voice was music to her ears, urging her to go even faster. Her hair danced back and forth, tickling her bare skin. Sergio grabbed her hair with both hands and pinned the golden locks to her head. He moaned loudly, his gruff voice rough against her eardrums.

Brianna shut her eyes so all she could stare into was a sea of black. This way, there was no sight in the way of her pleasure. Beneath her, she could feel Sandler squirming. Was this Sandler trying to get some of the pleasure? She could have sworn he was rocking his body in an attempt to rub her pussy. Maybe he actually was, and it intensified her pleasure. She moaned, a wave of adrenaline stealing over her. Her eyes squinted open and she glanced at Sandler. She winked at him and returned her attention to the huge cock she was sucking.

Sergio stabbed his way toward her throat. She didn't object. She held his cock in place and didn't back away when the gag reflex came knocking for the first time. With him deep inside her mouth though, choking her with his huge cock, it was impossible to breathe.

The second gag reflex, much more overwhelming than the first, had her pulling away from him. She took him in her mouth again, this time, she wrapped her fingers around the base of his cock. She looked up at him, holding his gaze as she sucked him. Sergio was breathing hard, his chest rising and falling. She didn't need to place a hand on his chest to know just how fast his heart was thumping. She could see from his flaring nose that he, just like her, had to give in to an overpowering surge of adrenaline, letting it flood his insides.

"Fuck, Bri! I'm gonna cum!" he groaned, his cock pulsating inside her. "Want me to cum all over him, eh?"

Brianna smiled, considering Sergio's idea. "He's all yours then."

She chuckled, her eyes fixed on Sergio as he pulled out of her and mounted the bed to stick his cock inside Sandler's mouth. Sandler clamped his mouth shut and flung his head to the side.

"Come on now," Brianna said. "Be good! Well, as I said, if you're good I'll keep this little porn clip to myself, but if you're not…"

She smiled, watching Sandler's lower lip reluctantly fall open. She'd known he would comply. He wouldn't want his porn video circulating the Internet. She bit her lower lip to trap in a bubble of laughter as Sergio stroked himself just above Sandler's face. And then, with a growl, Sergio rained down cum on Sandler's face, marking him like the shameless sissy that he was. Globs of cum dropped into Sandler's mouth.

"You know better than to spit that out!" Brianna said,

stopping him from spitting.

He made a face and gulped it down. More drops of cum rained down on Sandler's face, and when it was all over, Sergio shook off the rest of his cum.

Brianna sat on Sandler's torso the whole time, watching him swallow. "You're quite a swallower. Good job."

"Please," he begged. "Make this stop. Just tell me what you want, Brianna."

"To see you submit yourself like a loyal dog." She leaned toward his face and whispered, "By the way, do you know this song with the lyrics 'bottoms up'?"

Once the last phrase rolled off her tongue, she stuck out her ass and buried her face in the crook of Sandler's neck. She grabbed her left ass cheek with her left hand and moved it sideways, away from the other ass cheek. Her fingers slipped through her ass crack to tease her dripping wet pussy. The groaning bed told her of Sergio's presence behind her. She bit down on her lower lip, awaiting the stab of his cock. She stiffened as his huge cock kissed her asshole, and then he slipped past the tight hole, finding warmth between her pussy lips.

She cried out. "Yes, oh fuck! Deeper, please!"

She grabbed Sandler's shoulders and squeezed tight. She moaned and cried as Sergio reached deeper, and although her voice was too loud for Sandler's comfort, she made no attempt to adjust her pitch.

"Fuck, Sergio! You're a man! You're a real fucking man!" she gasped, trying to catch her breath. "Oh yes, harder!"

"Love it when I fuck you so hard, huh?" Sergio asked, his voice shaky as he pounded harder.

"Yes, yes, yes! I fucking love it! Oh Sergio, you feel great inside me. So fucking great!"

Her pussy sloshed and clenched, her ass rocking back and forth. Sergio grabbed her hips, and then he slammed so hard, she collapsed on Sandler.

Sandler groaned from the impact.

"Damn it Sergio!" Brianna cried. "You are so good! So fucking good!"

She hummed, and then she clamped her lips together. In the absence of words, she kept humming, deep moans erupting from her clenching stomach.

"Oh fuck it feels so good when you fuck my pussy like that!" she cried. "Sergio…"

"Mmmh baby?"

"Cum inside me..."

She reached for Sandler's neck and wrapped her fingers around it. Her fingers tightened around his throat, only easing up when she felt him stiffen, two veins stretching down his forehead as he tried to breathe. She let go of his neck and he gasped for breath, his nose flaring.

"Oh fuck!" Sergio cried out. "Here it comes!"

He thrust harder, deeper, faster. And then, he growled, emptying himself.

Brianna stuck out her ass some more, thrusting back to pin herself to Sergio's body. He was sweaty despite the air condition in the room. She was just as sweaty, her body gliding along with Sandler's as she thrust back and forth.

Sergio pulled out of her, his hands gripping her waist. He reached down and planted a kiss on her ass.

"You're so full of me, baby," he said, spanking her ass.

"Time for someone to get to work," Brianna said with a smile. "Untie him, Sergio. Let's see if he has learned the ABC of submission."

She heaved herself off Sandler and lay on her back.

She parted her legs as she watched Sergio untie Sandler. The man would probably say no, refusing to lick her clean, but for his sake, she hoped he wouldn't.

Once untied, he got on all fours, his eyes finding the raw flesh between her legs.

He dove between her legs with a speed she hadn't seen coming. She gasped, knocked out of breath, but she quickly found her breath again. As though her legs weren't already parted, Sandler flung them further apart and buried his head between them. She whimpered at the first feel of his tongue on her sensitive skin, but she made no attempt to move away. She watched, her eyes gleaming with pleasure as he sucked her like a thirsty man who had just found a bottle of water after a lifetime in a desert.

Fuck the divorce, Sandler, she thought. I should tame you instead.

She smirked, loving the sound of that. Prior to now, she had never thought of taking the reins of their marriage. Now though, after having a taste of what it felt like to be the one in control, with so much power at her disposal, she concluded that this was just how it was meant to be. It was only a matter of time before her narcissist of a husband became a proper sissy, living to serve her.

With a satisfied smile, she parted her lips, letting Sergio fill her mouth with his cock once again.

The First Threesome Relationship

It was one of those dead moments in court, in which you have nothing to do but wait for your turn. Luckily for me, I was with Jasmine, who liked to tell me anecdotes about her sex life, without ever leaving out the details. That day was no different, describing her first threesome relationship in high school style note passing, which as was easy to imagine, was anything but normal.

The story went like this, "As soon as I finished high school, my mother decided to reward me with two weeks at the seaside, in the company of her friend Amber's family, who at the time had a small house near Jones Beach. Amber had a son, Alex, whom I had not met for years. He remembered meeting me, but I didn't remember him. Of course, that could have been because it had been at least 12 years since we had seen each other and he was now 20 and I was 18 and a half. He seemed like a total nerd; he was always with a book in hand.

"Alex was also rather ugly, as well as physically frail and with thick coke bottle glasses. On the other hand, he was immediately very kind to me, taking me to the beach when we met. Among them was Connor, whom to call beautiful is, to say the least, simplistic, a true

Adonis. All the girls at the beach were into him. But Connor was very reserved, almost giving the impression that he found the attention of the girls annoying, giving them over to Alex and another boy.

"During the first days of vacation, I noticed that every now and then Alex and Connor disappeared for a few hours, but I didn't give any importance to the fact, intent as I was to look for some nice boy to have sex with. One day; however, I had a small accident while talking to some girls, and I spilled my drink on my bathing suit, staining it, so I decided to go home to change.

"As I arrived in front of the door, I saw the bicycles of Armando and Connor, and in my naivety, I thought they were in my friend's room looking at some porn videotapes. So, I went in silence heading towards his room, where I entered without knocking and finding myself in front of a scene that shocked me. Alex was lying on the bed intent on giving his friend a blowjob.

"As they saw me the two turned white, looking for sentences, to say the least incredible, to justify themselves.

'You're just a couple of homos,' I said, pointing to them with my hand.

'No, it is he who is gay,' Connor said 'I'm just me. I don't believe in labels like that. '

'First, you take a blowjob from a male, and I bet you also put it in his ass!'

'It is true, but what can I do? Your friend is a slut of the highest magnitude.'

'But don't you like vagina,' I asked him, taking off my shirt and my bikini top.

'Come here, I'll show you what I don't like,' he replied, smiling.

'First, let me have a good time with the big boy,' I knelt in front of him and took out his hard shaft. He was flaccid but as I started licking him from the base of his balls to the tip, he eventually grew in size. When it was finally fully erect, I took it in my mouth.

'Look at your friend,' said Connor 'She is almost sluttler than you! Today, I'm going to screw you both.'

"Alex eventually greedily took Connor's penis from me and sucked his manhood like he had something to prove.

"Finally, Connor said to me, 'Jasmine, what are you waiting for, get undressed. I bet you have a fabulous ass.'

"So, I took off my shorts and slipped off my bikini bottoms, and as he approached me, Connor put his hand on my butt, feeling it with force.

'But look at you how wonderful! I bet you've definitely taken dick before. Maybe not as many as your childhood friend. Who knows how many shafts he takes at the university. While at New York State College, I bang a forty-year-old in front of her cuck husband and the more she has the most she wants.'

"In deep excitement, I lowered myself between his legs and licked his balls, while Alex continued to suck him like a true whore. At that point, Connor took my friend's head and literally started hammering him in the mouth, calling him the worst epithets that can be said to a homosexual.

'Connor, what do you say we send this boy to ecstasy,' I said, seeing my eager friend wanting to be screwed.

'Okay, I'll bang him,'

"Alex, who had not opened his mouth since I entered his room, waited for me to lie down on the bed, to get on top of me. As he settled in, his friend opened his buttocks and penetrated him with a sharp and firm blow.

'Not too hard,' protested Alex, who was immediately silenced by Connor.

'Shut up, bitch, once you get it, you will never want me to stop doing you.'

"In fact, my friend's penis became even harder and swollen, and it didn't even faze him when I started to suck it.

'You're two demons,' exclaimed my friend. "I'm going to enjoy this so much."

'And you lick my snatch,' I replied a little angrily. 'You don't want to be the only one to enjoy such a prick.'

"Actually, Alex was being banged so hard by his friend that he could barely focus on my center of pleasure. Meanwhile, I gave him the blowjob of my life, occasionally making a pass at licking Connor's testicles, in hopes it would soon be my turn.

"The pig amused himself by pushing my friend's ass a couple of times to my mouth as he continued to screw him with his thumb, which he rotated inside him, making him moan even louder.

'Come on, lay down so your whore friend will ride you a little and let's see if you can suck me,' he told him suddenly without removing the big finger from his ass.

"Alex obeyed timidly, then I climbed on him, making his penis disappear between my legs.

'But look at that nice couple of sluts,' exclaimed Connor approaching us 'Now give me a nice blowjob, so that I really enjoy this.'

"Like a bolt I threw myself on his penis, leaving the balls to my friend, who took to them like it was his job. While I tried to take the right time between the two boys, so they could both enjoy themselves, Connor jumped onto the bed, quickly putting himself behind me.

'I don't even care if you are a virgin from behind, whore like you who knows how many knobs you took and how much cum has filled this great ass,' he said spreading my buttocks with his hands.

'Wait up! No two together,' I shouted with a smile to let him know that I was just protesting like good girls should. I even managed to fake an attempt at trying to slip away.

'Two together, yes,' he replied pushing the head inside my little hole.

"I shouted like the devil, but he continued to screw me paying no attention to my feigned complaints, I let him do it waiting for the moment when the pain would turn into pleasure. When that happened, I started shouting, losing every inhibition and tried to incite the two boys to do their best.

'It is beautiful! I've never felt so full. Alex try and be a little more manly like your friend, the stallion.

'But I ... really ... I can't move,' my friend mumbled.

"To try to give him extra energy, I put his tongue in his mouth, but soon I had to take it off because the lunges from Connor were so violent.

'You're more of a whore than your friend,' The stallion whispered in my ear. 'At least he takes dicks one at a time.'

'I bet he can't wait to get double penetrated in the ass,' I replied smiling. 'It's not my fault if he only has one hole.'

"Connor continued to hammer into me until he was close to orgasm, then he made my friend and me kneel next to each other, to masturbate in front of us.

'I'll bukkake you sluts,' he shouted shortly before cumming on our faces.

"When Alex and I ended up removing Connor's seed from our faces, licking it eagerly, I decided to get my friend to come.

'Come, let's finish this. I'll empty your balls.'

'But you have no penis,' my childhood friend objected.

'You obey and don't go soft on me,'

" Alex got down on his hands and knees apprehensively, but he changed his mind when I began to eat his ass and soon he realized that I was sodomizing him with four fingers.

'So, it's true that you really are an asshole,' I jokingly told him, grabbing his penis to masturbate him.

'Yes, I can do it. I like taking it in the ass. And the more I get, the more I want.'

"My friend came quickly, filling my hand with his cum, but I didn't have time to clean up when Connor pushed me onto the bed making me fall with my legs open.

'Now, I'll screw you, I want a vagina,' he said, putting himself on top of me.

'Shut up and fuck me,' I replied, making him feel my nails lightly on his back.

"The boy proved to be a real stud, surely the 'lessons' he had in with the forty-year-old woman taught him to make the woman he was with really enjoy every thrust, unlike the anal, this time he didn't only think of his own pleasure. Connor took me in all possible positions, making me have an orgasm almost immediately, and then arriving together with the next, while he was screwing me from behind. He came on my back.

" Alex lapped it up like a hummingbird looking for nectar; which, he then wanted to share with me. I spent the rest of the vacation having sex with those two guys, and only the evening before leaving, Alex left me alone with Connor, we had a marathon of sex inside the cabin that my aunt had rented for the summer.

"We left the next day with a promise to see each other again as soon as possible, but as often happens, several years passed before this could happen," Jasmine finished her story and shortly thereafter a text message arrived on her cell phone. "I have to go, my trial is starting," she said, picking up her things.

"But how do you know when it's your turn," I asked curiously.

"Just do a couple of blowjobs where you need to and you get a little extra help, simple right?"

I laughed seeing her leave, knowing full well that she hadn't lied to me about anything.

A Rough Gangbang

Lucy is sick of being prim and proper and made to be a good girl by her father who is a Man of God. She's ready to rebel in the biggest way for her first time. She gets an opportunity and she takes it. She visits the bad side of town. Now she's in the dark world of the biker gang and in their lair. But Lucy isn't scared. This rebellion is the best thing she's ever done and she's certain there's over fifteen bikers who agree.

I was angry and bored, but mostly angry. Once again I have to miss out on the fun. I'm twenty years old, and Papa still won't give me a second of freedom. I've had it with being preached to. "While you're under my roof it's my rules. If you sin, you won't go the Heaven. The devil is everywhere, and temptation will lead to ruin."

I had to study, study, study. I had to get the best grades. I had to attend bible studies. I was only allowed out with other Christian young ladies and with a suitable adult chaperone. This was ridiculous. If I could find a job somewhere, I'd run away and never have to come back near Papa again.

I'd go and find Mama who'd left five years go and said she couldn't take me because she couldn't afford to educate or care for me properly as she wasn't sure how long it would take her to get on her feet. But she'd come back for me as soon as she did, she promised. Yeah right. She might be dead now for all I knew. Last I heard was that ear-breaking roar of a motorcycle taking her out of town.

I didn't blame her. She'd found a way out and taken it. I would do the same thing if I could. Papa was so devout, so single-minded, so crazy with being Christian, he was impossible to reason with. He used Mama as the perfect excuse for what could happen. She'd let the devil had his way, she wasn't strong enough to resist, she was hell bound. Blah, blah, blah.

From where I sat the tattooed, long-haired, muscled man on the cycle was the Savior. I wish I'd gone too. I wish I'd been old enough to get on the back of a motorcycle and disappear. But here I sat, bible in hand, trying to make sense of how long I had to be this miserable for. It was my twenty-first birthday next month, and I didn't want to spend it with tea and cakes at the church ladies' idea of a party.

What I needed for my birthday was freedom. Freedom and fun. Fun like the women have in the books I read under the covers at night and then hide in a secret compartment in my cupboard. If Papa found them, he'd be out of his mind. I'd felt the sting of his strap before, and I didn't want to again. When he flipped out mad, there was no telling what he'd do in the name of the Lord. He gave God a bad name.

I'd read my share of the bible and from I could see, God and Jesus were about forgiveness and not being perfect. Being kind to others, and treating people the way you want them to treat you. I couldn't see how dressing a certain way made you a sinner. It was crazy.

I was over begging Papa to let me go. It wasn't happening, and I'd just say I had another headache if anyone asked, which they wouldn't. I was invisible to everyone at that school. I doubt they'd even know I was gone if I died tomorrow. Right now, I was over this awful life and being so unhappy.

I had to do something about it, but what? I didn't want to steal from anyone to get money to leave. I wasn't really sure what I could do to support myself. I wasn't sure I had any talents at anything except school, plus I had one more year to finish my degree in religious studies. Not that I was really interested in that, but Papa had let me choose any minor, and I'd been studying drama.

I wanted something I could use when I left here. I just had another year to go. How I was going to get through that year, I didn't know. I had to find a way. I needed an outlet. Papa wouldn't let me do anything that wasn't associated with the church and with me heavily under guard. So I'd also need to be creative. Sitting here bored wasn't the most fun.

I'd told Papa I didn't feel well, and he'd left me to go to his weekly meet up with other Pastors in our area. He'd be gone most of the day, and I'd taken the day off school from illness. He'd be home early for sure because I was here alone. So that gave me roughly five hours, and I wasn't going to find any fun on this side of town.

I stuffed an outfit into a bag and my disguise items and walked the block to the library. They had study room I could book out for the whole day. One of them also had a nice sized window into a back alley. I had the same tight outfit similar to what many of the other girls at Uni wore and a black wig, oversized sunglasses and makeup. In particular, a deep crimson lipstick... It made my mouth look amazing.

Even if all I did was walk around feeling normal for two hours, I'd be happy. Anything had to be better than the neck to ankle outfits I wore every day. No makeup, plain hair, boring clothing. I felt about ready to burst. There was so much inside me dying to get out. If I didn't let off some steam, I'd just have to run away for good. But one more year and I could go and do whatever I'd studied so hard for, be an actress. Today, I'd go and be the Lucy I want to be and not the one I'm forced to be. I wasn't just going to read about how it felt to be loved, I was going to find out, somehow.

****

The other side of town, the sinful part, looked much the same as where I lived. Houses, stores, apartments. Sure, there were a few more people on the streets, but it didn't feel particularly dangerous. But lunch time was hardly likely to be pumping. I sighed, it was all the time I had so I'd still enjoy myself.

The warm summer air touched all the bared parts of me and felt divine. I imagined it was a hundred different hands caressing my midriff, my thighs, my cleavage. I had a strange, exciting feeling swirling inside me and between my legs, it felt like extra blood was pumping. I'm not expert, but I'm pretty sure I'm sexually aroused. It was exhilarating to feel so free.

I had a sexy book in my bag. I liked how romances all had happy endings, it gave me hope. I also liked the raunchy, bad-boy hero in this one. He talked dirty and knew how to back up the words. I blushed almost the entire book, but I'd brought it along to read again today. Papa would die if he knew what was available in the libraries these days.

I found a park and headed to a park bench facing the road. I didn't want to miss any action, never know when my hero would show up. I grinned and crossed my long legs, leaning back a little. I was going for the sexy, lounging look. My head was hot from the wig though, and I doubted anyone who really knew me would be near here, so I pulled off the black wig and shook my long bangs free.

I was just into one of my favorite sex scenes in the book, and deep male voice spoke beside me. I jumped and quickly stashed my book in my bag. Shit, I had to work on being less guilty.

"You're Lucy, right?"

I looked at him, he looked familiar somehow. Around his eyes or his face. But I'd never seen anyone with so many tattoos up close. His dark hair was rough, and tumble and his blue eyes sent a jolt through me. How the Hell did he know my name? I just stared at him through my sunglasses.

" It's Lucy, from drama class, I know it is. I'm Jason…We were in a group together at the beginning of the year. Did the work on body language. I look a little different." He pulled his log fringe back and pulled his hair up into a small bun on top of his head.

Now, I knew I'd seen him before. He was quieter than me. He looked anything but quiet right now.

"Jason…wow. You look totally different."

He grinned, and that sent a thrill over me and let his hair flop down again. I'd never had a man give me a smile like that before.

"You're the one who's different. Fuck, you're hot as."

Showtime. Now was my chance to put my acting skills to work. I'd never flirted before. I took off my sunglasses and gave a big smile.

"Are you here with anyone?"

I shook my head. "No. I'm here looking for some fun."

He frowned. "I'm not sure you should be joking about that around these parts."

"I'm not joking, Jason."

"Look, everyone around here calls me Tank."

"Okay, Tank."

"Ya wanna grab a beer? I know a place where you can get some fun, I'll keep an eye on you."

I could hardly tell him I'd never tasted beer. "Sure. I'd love to. My bus leaves in two hours."

"I'll get you the bus stop."

"Let's go then."

"I tone down who I am during class. Bikers don't belong in drama."

"Well, the pastor's daughter doesn't belong on the wrong side of town either but here I am."

"What kinda fun you lookin' for? Cos where I'm takin' ya, if you put it out there more than one ape is gonna pick it up. Might be a fight until you choose."

"Maybe I won't choose. Maybe I'll like them all." My words surprised me, but I had to admit the thought of more than one man touching me had me wet. It wasn't a virginal thought, nor a Christian one, but I had to maximize today, I didn't know if I'd ever get another chance. I wanted to see what sex was like. This was risky, I knew…but I trusted Tank.

Tank held his hand out to me. "C'mon. Let's see if you're bluffin'. But if you change your mind at any time, you let me know, and I'll get you outta there."

I nodded. "Sure."

"Time for this little girl to grow up. Your daddy keep

you hemmed in?"

" Papa never lets me breathe." I grabbed his roughened hand, it engulfed mine, and he dragged me up to standing.

His arm went around me and his lips crushed mine. My first kiss and I didn't have a clue. He seemed to sense my shock and backed off a little, his lips seeking mine in a less urgent way. His caressed my ass and kept me close to him. I opened my mouth to him, and his tongue eased inside, teasing and tasting.

I collapsed into him with the deliciousness of it all. He held me up against him, and I fit into the shape of his hard, sculptured muscles like a belonged there. He broke the kiss, and I whimpered at the loss.

"You done this before, Lucy?"

I shook my head.

"Fuck, girl. If I go back there with a woman as needy to be fucked as you, I'll have a fight on my hands. I can't hold them all off. They're animals."

"So don't."

"You don't know what you're saying. They'll pass you around like a cigar."

"I want to try it, if you're there to see I'm okay."

"I'll be there alright. I'll get you back home too. I'm not sending you by bus, and anytime you want any more fun, I'll come get you."

I nodded and smiled. Finally, I was being taken seriously. He took my hand in his. "Here, feel this. You'll have a lot of hard cocks to deal with."

I rubbed over his erection through his black leather pants and my pussy throbbed hard. I wanted him right here and right now. I needed to be fucked hard like the heroine in the book I'd been reading. My heart jumped in fear, but I was more excited than scared. I squeezed him, and he groaned. "Over here."

He took me into the wooden shelter. "We have to hurry, Lucy. People come through here all the time on their way home from work. Just a quick taste of what to expect. I'll get you ready. Relax for me, Baby. Trust me and give yourself over to the pleasure."

He kissed me again, insistent and demanding. I let myself g with the feeling and kissed him back the same way. He growled into my mouth, and he touched between my legs, up under my short, tight skirt to the flimsy underwear beneath. I sucked in a deep breath because it was like nothing I'd ever felt before. He stopped kissing to speak in a deep, rasping voice. "Put one foot up onto the bench seat. Open wide for me. Let me feel how wet you are; how fucking tight I know you'll be."

I did as he asked and he pushed the thin strand of silky material aside. He touched my gently along my pussy and dipped into my folds slightly. As he worked his way up, I braced myself for the contact. Nothing could prepare me for the electricity when he touched my clit. I cried out, and he laughed. He circled my opening. I felt myself clench at the slight contact.

"Has anything ever been inside you, Lucy?"

"No."

"Not even your own finger?"

I shook my head.

"Oh, Babe…That fucking blows my mind. I've never had a real first-timer before. You scared?"

I shook my head and undid his button and zipper. His cock was free, and the size of it shocked me. I imagined it inside my aching pussy. "Fuck me." The bad words tasted good in my mouth. "Show me what it feels like to come."

He was a little taller than me and three times across the heavy shoulders. His huge muscles flexed under my touch. I moaned in pleasure when he circled my clit faster and everything inside me tightened.

He bent his knees a little. "Widen a bit, Baby. This will hurt, but It'll feel so good very soon."

I made it easier for him to place the head of his cock at my entrance. He still played with my clit, and I braced my hands on his shoulders for balance. I was sure I'd collapse any second from how aroused I was.

"You're sure?" he asked.

"Yes, I'm sure. Hurry."

He stopped playing with my clitty and guided his cock to press right at my entrance. The pressure was amazing, and it did hurt a little but wanted more. I thrust my hips forward, and the head of him breached me. He swore under his breath and held still. "Are you okay?

"Yes, don't stop. Fuck me."

"You're killin' me here, Lucy. You're so tight around me, I think I'll explode before I get halfway." He looked hard at me then. "Wait." He pulled out of me. And moved apart a little diving his hand into his back pocket. "We need this. No sex ever without one, okay?"

"Okay."

He dragged a condom on. "This'll help me hold back until you're ready to come."

"Okay."

Then he positioned me again and pressed his sheathed cock to my pussy opening which had clenched up even tighter like the rest of me in anticipation.

"Breathe out, Lucy. Deep breath in and then out, relax as you go."

I let out the breath I'd been holding without realizing, and he breached me again with his swollen cock. I sucked in a big breath, and as let it out slowly a let my body relax as much as I could. As I did, Tank pushed up inside me more, and I gripped his shoulders hard.

Yeah, it hurt. But it also felt fucking awesome. "More."

I sucked in another breath, and when I exhaled, he buried himself inside me, and I yelped a little and then groaned.

"Hold still, babe, someone's coming." I never moved and neither did Tank. His cock was hard up inside me, and I became accustomed to being filled for the first time. I heard conversation and footsteps as the people passed by, unaware I was being fucked right under their noses. I like the thought of that. The thought of someone watching drove me crazy. I moved my hips because I couldn't wait. I began fucking him faster.

"I'm going to give it to you now, pretty Lucy, you're ready. Put your legs over my hips. Wrap them around me, Babe."

"Yes, yes. I'm ready. So good. It feels so fucking good."

I wrapped my legs around his trim waist, and hip and his powerful thighs took my weight easily as he thrust up into me. I raked my nails down his shoulders, and he growled and cursed and fucked me harder. My clit rubbed against him as he was still hard up in me and I was grinding onto him.

"Fuck, Lucy. That's it, you're my bitch, You're gonna make me come now." His frenzied movements put me somewhere I'd never been and my whole body locked up and he drove into me over and over again, and I cried out for more and more. I couldn't get enough, and I never wanted it to end.

Together we shook and vibrated against each other as my very first orgasm ripped through me. It was better than I could ever have imagined. Tank took a few seconds and then pulled out of me. He zipped up and grabbed my hand. "Let's go."

I had my bag over my shoulder, and I followed him hoping for more of what I'd just had.

"Was I good enough?"

"The best. Now we're going to get some of what you really came for. More cock than you could ever imagine.

****

He was right. Inside the darkened bikers den, the bar had a few lights, and once my eyes adjusted, I saw about fifteen bikers and all of their eyes were on me. Tank held my hand and whispered in my ear. "You want out…you say the word?"

I shook my head. I've never been so scared in my life. This was by far the most dangerous thing any woman could do. But I wanted this so bad. I wanted to rebel against all of the rules and regulations I'd followed all my life.

"This is Lucy. Make no mistake she's under my care. She wants this, but if she says no at any time, I'll kill a man who doesn't stop. She has to be home in an hour and a half, and her daddy is a man of God, so let's not get her into trouble or she may not ever come back to visit us again."

The bikers looked on as if it was something they heard every day. But the gleam in their eyes and the licking of lips told me this might be a real treat for them.

"Make sure she's enjoying every bit of it. If she ain't comin' neither are any of you. Oh, and clean condoms if you're inside her anywhere. There's a shitload behind the bar in the cupboard. I'm the timekeeper, and I'll enforce rules with my fists."

He pushed me forward, and I wasn't really sure what to do. I didn't need to worry because the biggest one picked me up and sat me on the bar in front of him. He peeled off my little top and leaned in the kiss at my nipples.

Wow. I loved how that felt, and I stuck my breasts out and looked over at Tank. He nodded, and I saw he was stroking his cock in full glory and he winked at me. Another huge man had gone behind the bar and gotten out a big box of condoms on the bar and then he pulled my arm back behind me and began to kiss and bite down the side of my neck.

"No marks where her daddy can see them." Tank ordered.

The biker moved to my shoulder and nipped and sucked away at my skin there while the first one drew at my nipples with his lips and grazed slightly with his teeth. It wasn't long, and there were many male hands touching me all over and many mouths sucking my breasts and skin. So many hot kisses and tongues to taste I was in real Heaven. I ached for release again, and I closed my eyes and let out a loud moan.

"Lucy needs to come. Sort it out." Tank spoke again.

No one had touched my pussy, and yet I was wetter than before. A few of the leather-clad, muscle-bound naked men carried me smoothly to the pool table and sat my ass on the edge of that. Hands pulled my legs wide apart and supported them as the one and only clean-shaven biker smiled at me and stuck out the longest, thickest tongue I'd ever seen. He waggled it around and turned to the others. "Spread her legs and her cunt. Make that little pink clit pop out. Dr. Tongue is in town." His deep gruffness made me throb, and though I had no clue what he was saying, I just relaxed and went with it. Some of the others pushed me to lay down, and my arms were above my head.

My tits were getting another workout, and the long-tongued biker got on his knees between my legs. "Wider. Stretch her fucking wider." They did, and when his mouth went onto my pussy, I almost cried. Soon he was driving his tongue up inside me like it was a cock. But it was better because I could feel the movement of it deep inside and the pressure built. Then his huge tongue was on my clit, assaulting it every which way and then back inside me, fucking me again. All the hands on me and I writhed in the heat of it all.

"Joker, let her suck you."

A man who was slimmer, wiry and a little shorter than the others walked up to me with his cock hard and sheathed. It looked more thick than long, and when he offered me his cock at my lips I opened my mouth and thought the condom had a weird flavor at first, I soon got off on the feeling of a hard cock in my mouth while a tongue ate me out.

Hands were everywhere. Cocks were getting beaten off all around me as they watched me being handled on the pool table. I loved every second of it. I wish I hadn't waited so long. I knew there were fingers inside me now, it felt so different to the tongue, but he was onto my clit like an expert, and whose fingers buried inside me I didn't know, maybe more than one set, I was being stretched open more than Tank's cock and that was amazing. I wished I could get more inside me.

Me nipples were stinging, and I wanted more of that as well. My mouth was sucking cock, and just when I didn't think I could get any more done to me I heard Tank give an order, and it all seemed to build at once. The ones who were masturbating moved close to me, and they had no condoms. They were going to shoot cum all over me.

That thought tipped me over the edge and I cried out

as Joker pulled out of my mouth, ripped off his condom and began to jerk his cock hard over my face. I let go. I came what seemed like forever. Everyone seemed to cum at the same time as me. I had all their juices all over my body.

" Now fuck her hard. Smallest to biggest." Tank's orders came again. "Make sure everything is full when she comes next time."

I groaned and begged them to keep fucking me. I wanted it so bad and even though I'd had two orgasms I wanted more and I wanted every cock I could get inside me. Joker went first, and he'd put on a fresh condom, and they all did the same as he wasted no time fucking me as hard as he could. It wasn't long before he came again, and the next biker took his place. One after the other moved in, fucked me as hard as they could, and came.

I don't know how many it was, maybe twenty or maybe some came back for seconds, but when the last one moved between my legs, with my nipples and clit being teased perfectly, I looked down and gasped. I never saw this guy when I came in. His skin was darker, and he was built like a wall. His cock was so fucking big I didn't think it was possible to get that all in. No way. I tensed up, and Tank was by my side.

"You in or out, Babe?"

"Will it fit?"

He laughed. "You have no idea how good this cock will feel."

"Do it." I wasn't afraid enough to stop it yet.

Tank nodded at the huge man, and he grinned. The head of him was so massive it took a few minutes to get inside me but when he did, my eyes watered.

Soon enough I was begging for more, the pain was the best thing I'd ever felt. All hands and mouths were on all parts of me. That huge cock splitting me in half was the best thing of all. The intensity built again and this time, I was sure to explode into a million pieces.

My clit was being fondled perfectly and then my back arched high, and his huge cock slammed into me. I screamed, and the orgasm shattered me from the inside out. Over and over again I came. I was turned inside out. The bikers all swore, or cried out, or groaned my name and I felt so in control and powerful. I'd made this happen, I'd made them all cum more than once. Me.

Nothing had ever felt wonderful. My life was my own, and I got to forget about the shitty world I live in every day. I finally knew what it felt like to be happy and free.

A Student Day off

"Three, two, one, drink!" Four beer bottles and a wine glass rise into the air. The glass sounds and finds its way to the mouth. Four friends and I are sitting in this tight rented student room. Five used crates of beer stand against the wall with on the top box a collection of empty bottles of spirits. Opened bags of private brand chips complement the air of liquor and general mustiness. Today is Thursday — student day off.

"Trevor, do you want another one?" My bottle is dangerously empty. A nod is enough for Megan and she throws the next one to me. My group of friends in short everyone summarized: Megan is the diabolical activity starter who always manages to get out of trouble. Jeremy is the bulky, loud bat who likes to balance Megan's rope called problem without ever falling. Robert is the attempt at sobriety in the room. He provides an overview and unfortunately tries to play the father role failing. Lucy is the seemingly innocent girl, but because of her unreachable potential, she finds satisfaction in the few times she sees us, which often leads to wonderful escalations. And I, Trevor, am the boy who wants to get as much feeling as possible from an evening, good or bad.

"Come! We... To go... Step-puh!!" shouts Jeremy. We put our heads on our necks and we all produce a Huzaaa together. If someone had hung up a breath test in the middle of the room, you would get the effect of an elephant standing on a home-garden-kitchen scale. I empty the remainder of my beer, hit Lucy on the ass and walk to the bike. Behind me, I hear her whisper in a focused manner: "It felt good." A smile slides on my face. How wonderful if this can and maybe, although I am guaranteed to have a punch from her somewhere tonight...

The reason why Thursday is the student night is that other types of people cannot. The younger student, the working young adult, the working-to-old-before-going-out adult, on Thursday they are all offside. The entire entertainment strip is for the students. This generates coziness, uniformity and a kind of brotherhood. Even though we are all different, at the same time we look so much more alike than we think. Wait, am I saying this now, or is it my beer * hik * that speaks for me? Anyway, I still like a few.

We're at the club. The evening blends into the night unseen. Time is a concept detached from the alcohol-stunned brain. The only thing that matters is an experience. Feel the music pounding hard in your chest. Your energy must be an amplifier for a positive mood. The crowd on the floor will merge into one large social animal that is hungry for the feeling of feeling good. That animal is uncontrollable, because every cell of the animal leads its own life, at most influenced by its owner behind the turntable. One moment you feel connected to everyone. The other moment I am dancing sensually with Lucy alone. Everyone goes up in smoke around us. We stand opposite each other, hip-rocking and with bent, touching heads — my hands on her hips and hers on my neck. In her bright blue eyes, I read trust, pleasure. Going up in the moment I press her against me. Her face is hidden in my blouse. Her hands grab onto the fabric of my blouse by my key legs. Honest warmth and naughty pleasure fill my head. The naivety will want this moment not to stop.

The music track that matches the atmosphere created stops. The tone changes, as it will keep changing over and over again. The DJ says that the hands must be in the air. Slowly I let my hands go over her flanks, from bottom to top to the shoulders. It is a kind of temporary farewell. We laugh. Then Jeremy jumps on my back exclaiming: "Where are those hands! Jump! Jump! Jump! "And the self-constructed smoke curtain around us disappears. I try to jump with Jeremy on my back. We only hit three other people. Sorry, not sorry. I have the biggest smile on my face. Life is good.

Then I get eye contact with a beautiful girl sitting at the bar not far from us. Her gaze disappears towards her friend and then down to her plastic cup filled with a light blue drink. I am enchanted as I find my way through the crowd towards the girl. Heavy Jeremy on my back doesn't feel nearly as heavy anymore as long as I keep looking at her. I don't think anymore. Just before her, I put Jeremy down. She looks at me with an expectant look. Her finger plays with the top edge of her cup. I try to surpass the sound of the music when I ask in her ear if she and her girlfriend want to dance with Jeremy and me. She doesn't get me. I point at her, at me, on the dance floor. I do the same for Jeremy, her friend, the same dance floor. She taps her girlfriend and jumps off the bar stool. Jeremy looks at me briefly and I nod, which means: Come, enjoy.

The song that plays is a typical song for those who don't know how to dance and that are why it is explained in the text. Jump to the left. Jump to the right. Romance and intimacy die on such songs. Yet I stand hand in hand, eye to eye. We push ourselves away from the crowd. As if it is a style dance number, I train her in the directions tell. Her movements, her self-confidence, it increases with every measure that is played. Her shyness and restraint melt in the heat of the club. My gaze falls on her dress that plays with the male eye several times. Every time the material moves upwards through its conscious movements, it stops where its feminine secrets are hiding.

She sees what distracts me. She pulls away from me and dances one meter back. There she turns her back to me and sinks in one go through her knees so that her ass almost touches the beer-drenched floor. I'm sold. With her back still to me, I move to her. I close my arms around her waist and kiss her neck. Her hands glide through my hair. Two beautifully round buttocks rub against my half-stiff dick. Her head falls aside as a gesture saying: "Kiss me. Then kiss me. I want you — your warmth on my skin, this energy through my body. "Her soft skin is a canvas on which I work. Suppressed sighs near my ear, betray her excitement and pleasure. My hands frolic instinctively along with her breasts and slide down slowly. Both of us are sending so many signals that we want more. I spontaneously knead her hands-filling ass. A loud moan escapes her mouth. She releases herself and gestures at me and then the wardrobe: "Come with me."

We cycle in the earliest, cutting morning cold. Her name is Jennifer and she lives nearby. Isn't it crazy? The switch from the nightlife in which you feel happy with the illusion that everyone is completely euphoric, to the harsh reality of the world outside the club. The atmosphere is sexually tense. Our glances cross, make eye contact and move away to make room for a shared, excited smile.

The door slams shut. While I am getting ready to open my coat, Jennifer stops me. We face each other in silence and pull down my zipper. I'm being stripped. Hand in hand, she takes me into her room. She points to a chair and gestures me to sit. Little communication and yet we understand each other. Normally I like to take the lead myself, but so far I have been pleasantly surprised by her naughtiness. She sits on her knees in front of me and tries to loosen my shoes without losing eye contact. It is not going smoothly. It is precisely this stiffness in combination with her sweet smile that creates a clumsy situation that makes you feel human and pleasant.

Her long, slightly curly blonde hair drapes over her left

shoulder. Dancing and cycling have given her a rougher haircut. She sits on my lap. We lean towards each other and a gentle kiss ignites the calmly burning flame of desire. Our lips scan each other like emotional explorers in unknown territory. Then that flame ignites in a fierce sea of passion and lust — my hands around her lower back, hers on my chest. Our kisses are full of student love - short, furious and goddamn delicious. She gently bites my lower lip. As a counter-reaction, I kneaded her ass somewhat roughly. A sighed "hmm-yes" makes me smile stubbornly. She's one of them. Our mouths find each other again. Her lips keep answering my kisses. Deep, hidden desires are released. The mind longs for more physical pleasure.

"Get up a little, you want." Because of the space created, I can pull her dress over her ass and finally over her head. Young student tits in a deep red bra and a black slip challenge me. Reader, do you know imperfect perfection? It felt that way to me. As if it should be like this, here, in this room, with her.

She stands up and beckons with her index finger. Her fist grabs the top of my blouse and forces me to follow her playfully. She lets me walk back through her room until I come across a bare wall. For a moment, I am thinking of showing weakness by breaking our eye contact. I will play her power game, for now then. Button by button, she unbuttons my blouse. My torso and belly welcome the fresh air. I am breathing deeply; my chest rises. Just as she went down on her knees in the club, she now floats to the floor more slowly and rockingly. Her separated hands in my belt come together at my knot. She bites her lower lip as she pulls my pants over my butt, over my thighs, over my calves and ending at my ankles. I kick my pants away. Time to take over control...

Out of the blue, I lift her up by her thighs and lay her over my shoulder. A few nice blows land on her ass. "Oh hmmm," she approves. With my free hand, I unhook her bra, a little trick that often causes wonder. With a thud, I lay her on the bed and rid her of the deep red tits prison. Two beautiful, inviting nipples look at me.

I start my pillow tour with her jaw. With each kiss, I descend further south. I slurp her nipple on her neck, her breastbone and with strong suction — her back curves. My tongue is a shrinking tornado with the nipple as the eye. My other hand kneads the locked out tit. I gently roll her now wet nipple through my index finger and thumb to let Jennifer know how damn sensitive those pink meatballs can be. "Suck... again..." Her mouth is open when I take her stiff nipple in my pampered mouth. She raises her upper body to feel more — more, more, more.

Jennifer turns around. I'm lying down now. We share one French kiss and without general announcement, she pulls down my underpants. My pole stands its ground — a long lick from the bottom of my balls to the tip of my glans. Her mouth slides over my dick. I ram my head briefly into the mattress. What the hell did I miss this? Then I watch how she processes my dick and balls. Her fingertips gently massage my bag. She licks the entire perimeter from the bottom of my glans. With gargling sounds and lots of salivae, I can only imagine how much effort she makes for me. The gesture offends me. She tufts a good load of saliva on my dick and she plays my flute with loose wrists. Long strokes alternate with short ones and... Pfff... damn it... I have to focus not to get ready. Smacking noises and my accelerated breathing are the only noises in this room. I get it more than difficult. How Jennifer deals with my rock-hard cock, with speed and personal responsibility to make me feel good, I have a weakness for that — time to quickly turn the roles.

"Jennifer, wait. Lay down. I want to spoil you. "I am curious."Jennifer takes a pillow behind her back and with her legs spread, she welcomes me. Her black slip has an even darker black spot right in the middle. She's fucking horny. A little too enthusiastically, I grab her briefs and pull them away from under her ass. I hear a slight crack in the fabric and I catch myself with my impatience to make her come screaming. Instead of an angry look, she looks at me hopefully. "Trevor, do you want... do you want to handle me a little rough? I like that... "I had long picked up those signals from her, but I am grateful for her openness.

There has been enough foreplay. The drop that swings from her cunt to her anus is more than enough proof. Without warning, I let one big lick go down her cunt from bottom to top — quickly a few short, firm licks on her clitoris and her pelvis bounce up in this unexpected sexual wanted violence. With her eyes closed and mouth open, she turns to the ceiling. My tongue silently tells his story to the inner labia. The taste of her moisture is not good for many men, but it just kicks me — a kind of direct reward — a bear that wants to reach the last scraps of honey from the deep pot.

I bring a finger inside her. Almost without resistance, it slides into its last leg — a second one. "Did you say rough?" I am changing my body position. On my knees, I kneel beside her pelvis and put my second hand on her lower abdomen. This presses lightly on it. I tell her in a very monotonous way all these actions to soothe her attention. At a fairly fast pace, I don't move my fingers in and out of her now soaking wet cunt, but rather up and down, stimulating the g-spot enormously. Because of my hand on her lower abdomen, the feeling for her is only more intense. First, she tries to suppress her screams, but soon she doesn't succeed anymore. The whole student house will be jealous of this girl. Up and down, up and down. It sloshes and ripples in the hypersensitive cunt. She tries to get up, trying to escape my merciless fingers in vain. I quickly place one of my feet on her breastbone. With safe and conscious pressure, I keep Jennifer where I want her. Her power game at the beginning was sweet, but you shouldn't challenge me. Then I feel her pussy walls tightly contracting and relaxing. A surprisingly low moan follows along with a struggling body, unable to cope with this kind of pampering. You must know where the limits of your partner are. I feel that I have reached it with Jennifer. My fingers are spit out of her cunt with waves of sticky feminine moisture. I wipe most of it over her trimmed cunt, giving her those final stimuli. I flatter myself beside her and guide her physical and mental state to a point where the weather has fallen enough. Her body is shaking and she cannot utter a sensible sound.

"Ff-fuck, yes," she sighs.

Her beautiful eyes hold mine in a hold. Her hand rests on my somewhat sweaty chest. "Round 2?" I ask. "Come on," she looks at me in a challenging way.

She has regained her self-assured attitude. I lie on my back and she places my cock under her pussy. Would she be able to handle another round so soon, I wonder briefly? But my thoughts are interrupted when she jumps down at once. Time and again, I feel her body pound against my pubic bone and I realize that she wants more. Every time Jennifer moves up, I give her that boost with my hips. I see my pole wet with the wetness. Her pipe arts were delectable, but a smooth pussy that surpasses very little. I notice that she is gradually increasing the pace. Her hands rest on my chest and she works on my dick. I feel like taking over control again. See what you think about this. I cross my arms around her back and push her against my chest. With my knees bent now, I can easily and with pleasure plunge into her. I am stripped, sucked, pulled off; I am very close to my own limit. "Jennifer, I'll be right away." "Then ram him in, I'll catch you up." Such a direct girl. And I start bumping. With long, hard strokes, I ram my hard, stiff-standing penis inside her — again and again and again and again.

A dull chatter with each thrust echoed through the empty room. I feel her stiff nipples against my chest. From deep in all my senses, I feel a violent orgasm coming. It starts banging softly, but soon it dominates my brain. Then Jennifer says the liberating words: "Come! Now-uu! "At the next shot, lightning flashes flash through my body. Squirting after squirting hot seed sprays her hungry cunt. Her cumshot is vibrating. Uncontrolled last knocks I still bring her pussy inside, but then I am completely mentally and physically empty. She moans and I hum — a sex symphony whose primitive instinct is the conductor.

She rolls off me and comes to lie next to me. Her hand

disappears between her legs. Fingers with my seed disappear in her mouth. "Ff tasting," she giggles. With her other hand, she is caressing my quickly sagging penis. At the same time, we mutter: "That was fucking great." We laugh. I give her a kiss, which she answers passionately.

At the same time, I feel a gloom coming up with me. In the kiss, I try to keep my two conflicting emotions separate from sadness and happiness. But I won't see her again soon. That is student life. There are memories of pleasure, but at the same time, there is so much more going on. From now on, we will be connected most purely and honestly. Because if you can deal with each other at its most primitive, then you have been able to share an experience with a good person.

The First Threesome

It all started two weeks ago on Thursday. I was in bed with my girlfriend and we were still chatting after a nice game of sex. We had a visit that evening and drank a lot. I no longer know exactly how we got there, but the conversation turned out to have a threesome. We had talked about this before; my girlfriend knew that it seemed cool to me and she herself was not hesitant about it. We decided that we would do it someday, but with a girl. But then the main issue came; who would it be and especially how we got her into it. We soon concluded that it would be difficult for me to arrange a girl. After all, it seems a bit strange when you approach someone as a boy and ask if she wants to have a threesome with you and your girlfriend. Not much later we were, therefore, visiting Jasmine's friends and acquaintances, looking for someone we would like to have a threesome with and who would like to. We soon discovered who the chosen one was; Emily, a fellow student of Jasmine. I had only seen her once before, but I liked what I remembered about her.

But now we were still asked how we would ask her. Jasmine said it was strange to ask her, so we had to think of something else. I had an idea and asked my girlfriend for Emily's number. She gave me the number and I sent a text message with only the text "threesome?" I put my phone away and soon I was asleep. The next morning we woke up at ten o'clock. I looked at my phone and yes, a text back.

"Who and what" was the text. I showed it to Jasmine and couldn't suppress a smile. "Boy and girl, 20 and 19" I texted back and it was waiting again. Not much later I heard my phone again and I read her text "coordinates and names, please." Slightly reluctant, I asked her via text message if she was seriously interested or if we would only make a fool of ourselves if we now would make known.

You could read in her next text message that she thought she was being ridiculed, but we seemed to know her, so we knew the answer. Now we put on the bad shoes and I texted back "Jasmine thinks you would."

It wasn't long before Jasmine's phone rang. It was Emily. After a standard start of the conversation, she asked if Jasmine might have given someone her number. My friend answered casually that she had given me her number. It was quiet on the other side. Emily turned out to be surprised and hadn't sought Jasmine. If we knew for sure that we wanted to do this, she wanted it. And if we wanted that, at least me. We agreed that we would contact us early next week for a date. And so the weekend passed. The whole weekend I couldn't think of anything else and I walked around half the day with a half-decked cock. How often had I fantasized about sex with two girls and now I would get the chance. I think I walked around all weekend with a big smile on my mouth. I was once glad that the working week started again, which meant another day less waiting! Monday and Tuesday passed slowly and on Tuesday afternoon I finally got on the train to Leiden. An hour later I was waiting for the bus at the station in Leiden. At that moment I couldn't think of anything else anymore and I was really horny. After a few minutes, the bus arrived and I boarded. It was not far from the station to Jasmine's room, so I rang the bell a little later.

I embraced my girlfriend and gave her a nice French kiss. I put down my backpack and took out the drink. That Monday I left home from the university and passed the liquor store and bought some drinks. Bacardi for me, a bottle of berry gin for my girlfriend and Martini for Emily. We put the drink in the fridge and we walked on to her room. We lay down on the bed and watched a little TV. It was only seven o'clock and Emily would not arrive until half past nine.

The tension literally rose by the minute. The more it went towards half-past nine, the more nervous I became. Would she come? Would it be nice? Would Jasmine like it? Would Emily like it? Mountains ask shots through me. When we received an SMS from Emily at half past nine I thought: now she will cancel it. It turned out, however, that her meeting had ended a little and that she would come an hour later. So wait another hour, an hour that passed very slowly. Finally, we heard the bell and Jasmine got up to open the door. Emily came in and greeted her with a few kisses. She hung her coat on the coat rack and went on to the bedroom where I was still in bed.

When she came in, she smiled at me, stooped and also gave me three kisses. She sat down on the bed and I got up to give her something to drink. In the beginning, the situation was a bit awkward and we talked a bit about our studies and vacations. After a while, there was enough drinking and the air was almost literally crackling. We all knew what was about to happen and everyone waited for another to make the first move. I decided to break the ice and crept closer to Emily, who was lying between Jasmine and me. I put my hand on her stomach and started to caress her. Emily now looked at Jasmine and said, "Okay, shall we?" Jasmine answered her question by coming closer and she pressed her lips to Emily's mouth. I watched it and I was very horny to see my girlfriend kissing this beautiful girl. With my hand, I went exploring a little further and stroked Emily's breasts under her shirt. She had really beautiful breasts — large and perfectly round. I heard a sigh escape from her as I stroked her nipple. When I took my hand there, the room was immediately claimed by Jasmine. She crawled on top of her, still intensely kissing her friend and now let go of all brakes. I now saw Jasmine's hands go over Emily's big breasts and vice versa. I also saw a few hands disappear under Jasmine's shirt. I kept watching how they kissed and touched each other and meanwhile, I did not leave the legs and buttocks of the ladies undisturbed. It wasn't long before Emily took off Jasmine's shirt and in response; she pulled Emily up to take off her shirt too. The bras immediately followed, so now I was in bed with two beautiful girls with the bare upper body. The girls finally found time to take their lips apart and started kissing each other in the neck.

Jasmine lowered her head even further and took Emily's tits in her hands and started licking them. I looked at Emily, who was sighing with her eyes closed. Emily's hands lay on Jasmine's hips and off and I saw a few fingers disappear under the edge of the pants. Apparently, she had already unbuttoned the pants because Jasmine's nice buttocks were already half in the air. I now sat down behind the two and started to lick Jasmine's butt and gently bite into it. With my hands, I slid to the button of Emily's pants and loosened them. I also unzipped her fly and I grabbed the pants by the side and took them off.

Emily now pushed Jasmine on her back and crawled on her, again kissing her mouth. I lay down next to them again and I saw Emily's big tits hanging down horny and leaning on my girlfriend's breasts. This looked really horny! With my right hand, I stroked Emily's back and slid down to her buttocks. In the meantime, Emily had closed her mouth around Jasmine's nipple and was sucking on it. I slid my hand into Emily's panties and kneaded her soft buttocks. She had a nice tight ass with wonderfully soft buttocks. Teasingly, I let a finger slide through her butt crack and because she was slightly lowered on her knees to reach Jasmine's boobs with her mouth, her ass was slightly raised in the air. Because of this, I could just feel her labia and every time I left it with a soft touch — every time I did that I heard Emily moan softly. After being so busy for a while I also saw Jasmine's hands go to Emily's ass and I have now left her the room to play with that nice ass. Jasmine immediately slid her hands into the pants and I saw her hands glide over the buttocks under the dust. I leaned over to my girlfriend's face and started kissing her.

She was pretty horny, I could tell by the kiss. When she is horny, she kisses quite violently and occasionally bites my bottom lip. So she did that now and I answered her teasing bite by also biting her lip gently. Emily now stood up and started pulling on Jasmine's pants. Jasmine lifted her butt from the bed and soon the pants lay on the already considerable pile of clothes next to the bed. Emily now began to kiss and lick her in her groin. I felt Jasmine's breathing speed up and she made short, uncontrolled movements now and then. I stopped kissing to watch Emily slowly provoke her tongue in the direction of my girlfriend's tiny cunt covered pussy.

As she slid her tongue over the fabric, Jasmine curled her back and sighed deeply. After this, Emily took off

Jasmine's panties and threw herself enthusiastically into the wet pussy waiting for her soft tongue. First, I looked calmly on my side, which was happening in front of me. It all looked very horny, my girlfriend with her legs wide with a nice girl in between who, apparently and to hear, delightedly. Emily too looked very horny like this. Her thick tits always just hit the bed while she was licking. Her ass was in the air — just a pity that she was still wearing panties. I decided to do something about it and I got out of bed and squatted behind Emily. I pulled her pants down so that her delicious ass was finally exposed. I leaned over and started kissing her on her buttocks and like Jasmine; I occasionally bit softly in her delicious meat. I pulled the pants further down so that I was looking at Emily's pussy.

What I could see from behind was that she had shaved her lips and left a line of pubic hair above, just like my girlfriend always had. I touched her pussy really well for the first time. I let my hand rise from her knee between her legs and the higher I got, the more warmth I felt and the harder I felt my dick beating. Arriving at her slit, I felt that she was pretty wet. I let my finger slide through her labia a couple of times and when he was well wet, I leaned him gently against her pussy and let him go inside a bit. Emily apparently liked it, because I heard her sigh and she pushed her ass back. I now made short fuck movements with my finger and pushed him further and further in this way. When my finger was completely in, I left it there for a moment and gently moved it around them again. I heard Emily's pussy dripping with this movement and I couldn't hold back anymore, I wanted to eat her now. I now sat down on my knees in front of the bed and brought my head toward her crotch. Emily realized what I wanted to do and she sank a little further through her back so that her wet pussy could now be seen through her buttocks. I stuck my tongue out and at the first touch; I felt a shiver go through her. Her pussy felt very hot and wet and I felt her lips drift apart when I licked her slit with my tongue. I grabbed her by her hips and made long strokes with my tongue over her pussy, from just below her line to just above her asterisk. I heard her sighing louder and louder and she pushed her ass further and further back so that at one point I was pressed against her with my whole face. Increasingly enthusiastic I started licking her and I also let my fingers do some work. I gently massaged the inside of her pussy while I continued to lick her. Occasionally I let my tongue go a little further and licked her ass, which caused a shiver at Emily every time. After a while, I saw Jasmine's legs tremble. She was coming ready.

I noticed from Emily's movements that she started to

lick more enthusiastically and when I took my mouth off her pussy I could see between her legs how she now flashed up and down with my finger in my girlfriend's pussy. I heard Jasmine sigh and groaned deeply. She bent her back, grabbed Emily's head and pushed it against her pussy. In the meantime, I continued to play Emily's pussy with my thumb, who was also breathing heavily. Suddenly I saw Jasmine relax and she let go of Emily's head. Emily sat up and I saw the two smiles at each other.

"Well, now it's your turn," my girlfriend said and pushed Emily away and crawled to her feet. She pulled the panties off her knees completely and pushed Emily's legs a little farther apart. The pussy that I had just warmed up was now ready for Jasmine. She no longer waited and put her mouth on the wet lips. I lay down next to Emily again and I looked at her. She had a horny look in her eyes and she smiled. I leaned over and started kissing her. She kissed very nicely, her warm tongue felt great in my mouth. During this kiss, I felt a hand of Emily sliding down my upper body. I was still here with all my clothes on; the girls were very mixed up so far; I was just not jealous. She put her hand on my crotch, where my dick had been locked up for a long time. She squeezed it gently and I couldn't suppress a moan. She now opened my belt and buttons with one hand. When she wanted to take my dick out of my pants, it didn't go so well, so I decided to give her a hand. I took off my pants and shirt and now, naked again, lay down next to her.

I started kissing her again and I felt her hand tightly close to my stiff cock. She slowly began to jerk me off; it was wonderful to see my girlfriend licking this horny girl while she pulls on my cock. It seemed that Jasmine was full of enthusiasm, I saw her make long strokes over the wet pussy and meanwhile making quick movements with a finger in it. Emily heard it audibly; she moaned rather loudly. This excited me even more and kissed her more violently. Not long afterward I noticed that she was breathing hard through her nose and interrupted her kiss. She came with loud moans. Jasmine kept on licking and there seemed to be no end to it. Eventually, Emily relaxed and she looked at Jasmine in horror.

Jasmine now noticed that I was in bed naked and she moved to me. She took my dick and licked my jerk. I sighed deeply; I was very horny. While Emily was still stroking my balls, Jasmine started to blow me delicious. I lifted my right arm so that Emily could come closer. She lay down on her side against me with her head on my shoulder. I was now sucked by my girlfriend, with another nice girl in my arms. I felt Emily's big tits lean against my body. I turned my head and started kissing her again. Suddenly I felt Emily moving a little and I saw that she had spread her legs a little. Jasmine had brought her free hand back to Emily's pussy and she was sitting in and out of it now. I closed my eyes again and enjoyed the blowjob and the situation.

I noticed that I didn't have to enjoy it that long because otherwise, I would be ready. I didn't want that. I sat up and motioned for Jasmine to stop. I thought it was time to fuck now. I turned Jasmine on her back and took a seat between her legs. I put my stiff dick in front of her pussy and slowly pushed him inside. She was very wet and she felt very hot. I kept sliding my dick a little farther in until he was completely in it. I let him sit like that and then started fucking at a slow pace. Emily was now again next to her girlfriend and started playing again with Jasmine's breasts. I saw her kneading those nice tits while she was singing with her tongue. I thought it was such a wonderful sight. For the umpteenth time that evening I felt happy. We fucked like that for a while and then I wanted to catch Emily. I took my cock out of Jasmine and moved something on my knees. Emily now spread her legs and looked at me horny. While I watched my girlfriend, I slowly let my dick slip into Emily's wet pussy. A deep sigh accompanied this. Even now I left my dick completely in her before I started fucking her. The roles were now reversed and Jasmine sucked on Emily's breasts again. I was so horny that I had to hold back half the time and concentrate not to get ready.

So I fucked her calmly and the other half of the time a little wilders. When I heard Emily moan louder and felt her cunt muscles tighten around my dick, I got too heavy and I knew I couldn't go back now. I was fucking her crazy now and I felt the cum crawling through my dick. I moaned loudly and squirted my seed into Emily's pussy. She kept moving her pelvis until my cock started to sag again. When I opened my eyes again and looked down, I saw two pairs of smiling eyes looking at me. I smiled at them and rolled on my side next to Emily. After soaking up for a while, we saw on the clock that it was now four o'clock. Since Emily had to get up at half past seven the next day to work, we decided to go to bed. After drinking a few large sips of water, we fell asleep with Emily between us.

Sex with the Professor

Ashton breathed out nervously as she stood outside the door to Professor Kingsley's room. In her hand, she held her books and folders which contained several tests, essays, and lab projects for the professor's Biology class; all of which were marked with failing grades. She shivered, nervous to confront the professor regarding her performance in his class. She was terrible at this subject, but she needed the basic credits in order to move forward in her college career.

Ashton knew this was possibly her last chance to save her grade and in turn, save her semester from being a complete and total disaster. She had a plan; or at least some semblance of one. It was a risky move for sure, but she hoped her good looks mixed with the knowledge that he was a single man would make things easier.

She extended her arm to knock on the door when it suddenly opened. There before her stood Professor Kingsley. He was a beautiful older gentleman, with salt and pepper hair and rugged features. He looked down at Ashton with his keen green eyes.

"Miss Thompson, what can I do for you?" he asked in his soft but stern voice.

"Uhm, uh," Ashton stumbled on her words. She was always very attracted to how handsome Professor Kingsley was, but she was also intimidated by him and his stern demeanor. She never had very personal interactions with him before considering he taught her in class of about eighty students, though he was the subject of many of her fantasies. "I was wondering if you didn't mind taking a moment to talk with me about my grades."

Professor Kingsley nodded and looked around the empty hall curiously before stepping back and welcoming Ashton into his office. She stepped in nervously and smile as he gestured for her to take a seat. She walked over and sat down quietly across from his desk as he closed the door and moved back to his chair.

"All right, Miss Thompson, you're here because you want me to tell you how you can not fail my class, is that correct?" he asked her in his deep, booming voice.

"Y-yes sir," Ashton squeaked nervously.

Professor Kingsley looked at her and sighed as he sat forward at his desk and proceeded to type on his computer. "Well, Miss Thompson," he started.

"Ashton, sir," she interrupted. "You can just call me Ashton."

Professor Kingsley nodded. "Ashton, I do appreciate you actually coming and expressing concern," he said. "You would be surprised how many students will flunk out of my class without ever attempting to better their grade or work towards extra credit. Many will just not show up to the final exam, without realizing that it is worth fifty percent of their entire grade."

Ashton breathed out with some relief as Professor Kingsley's voice softened immediately with her. She looked at him as he continued to type and thought curiously to herself. He really was a very handsome man, perhaps he would be willing to go easy on her through other means besides extra work. Ashton really hated Biology and it had always been her weakest subject. If he was this easy to have open up, perhaps she could convince him to open up some more and give her a real passing grade without taking the focus away from her other classes.

She looked down at her button-up blouse and continued to ponder. Thinking quickly, she reached up and popped off the top two buttons, giving a better view of her well-defined cleavage and the outer lining of her bra. Ashton had thought about seducing a teacher before but was never brave enough to go through with it. She was always very attracted to older men, and she didn't want to admit that part of the reason she was failing Professor Kingsley's class was because she was too busy admiring him and his rugged good looks.

She leaned forward on the desk to make sure her chest was plenty visible. "Anything you could do to help me, or anything I could do to help you help me," she said. "That would be fine with me."

Professor Kingsley turned his head to look at her and immediately his eyes were drawn to the beautiful, lightly freckled skin of her breasts as they looked to nearly pop out of Ashton's blouse. He cleared his throat and sat back, looking at Ashton with unsureness as to what to say.

"Miss Thompson… Ashton," he clarified. "Am I to assume you came to me with a planned course of action?"

"No sir," said Ashton as she gave him a kind smile. "It's more of a spur of the moment thing."

Ashton could see in his eyes that he had reservations regarding what she was implying, but he couldn't bring himself to look away from her chest and say no. Ashton's heart was pounding with excitement at the mere thought of fulfilling a fantasy with her most handsome professor. She bit her lip and stood slowly, acting more now on impulse than critical thought. She stood up and quickly locked the door before strutting around to the professor's chair with her fingers lightly following the outer edge of the desk.

"A spur of the moment?" he asked her.

"You don't believe me?" Ashton asked. She didn't want to come off as a slut, but she knew this was her one and only chance, as Professor Kingsley was surprisingly receptive to her advances. She set the books and folders she had carried with her on his desk and dropped to her knees, falling right into his lap. He looked down at her nervously as he double-checked the door to the room was locked. "It's okay, I locked it," she reassured him.

"You know, I wasn't implying you had to do any of this," said Professor Kingsley as he watched Ashton pull down his zipper.

"Trust me, professor, I wouldn't be doing this unless I wanted to," Ashton said. "If it will help you think of a way to let me pass your class, then all the better, right?"

"I'll think about it, of course," said the professor. Ashton breathed out nervously but smirked to hide her unsureness. She reached her hand into his pants and could feel his growing cock. She gasped as she pulled it out and watched it grow in her hand. Without another thought, she closed her eyes and went down, taking all of him into her mouth. Professor Kingsley watched and gasped with surprised pleasure. "You're making a very good argument for yourself right now though, Miss Thompson."

"I'm way better at Anatomy than I am Biology, Professor Kingsley," said Ashton as she came up from sucking on his firm rod.

"I can tell," he said with a relieved sigh.

Ashton was excited that Professor Kingsley enjoyed her argument for leniency with her grades. She felt him quiver and throb in her mouth. It was clear he was really enjoying this. She sucked harder as she let her warm, wet tongue caress his rigid shaft. Her heart pounded with excitement as she suckled hard on the tip of his head and drew her first taste of pre-cum. He tasted savory and sweet, not salty like she would have expected. Of course, he looked like a man who maintained a very healthy and rich diet. The professor put his hands down gently on her head and started to rub his fingers through her thick strands of auburn hair.

"I do think you are a very beautiful young woman," the professor whispered to her as she continued to deep-throat him.

She couldn't help but smile with his cock filling her mouth. She continued to suck as her fingers moved along the line of his belt and slowly undid the buckle. She wanted to take the professor the whole way if she could, as that would be all of her fantasies coming to full fruition. Professor Kingsley did not stop her. In fact, he helped by slowly undoing the buttons of his shirt and loosening his tie.

Ashton's heart raced with adrenaline as she couldn't believe how this turned out. She looked up to gander at the well-defined muscles of the professor's chest. It was hard to tell how fit he actually was under the suit uniform he always wore. He reached out and slowly pushed against Ashton's shoulders. Ashton breathed out as she pulled all of him out of her mouth and took the hint to stand for him.

The professor examined her with great admiration as he guided his hands around the fine curves of her body. He pulled up on her blouse, removing it from the tucked position in her skirt and pulling it over her head. Ashton felt herself become more and more wet with anticipation as she shivered from his gentle touch.

The professor pulled her closer to him, his cock still fully erect out of his pants. Ashton could feel it as it poked under her skirt. She blushed knowing that this was going to be a moment unlike any other, going all the way with the admirable Professor Kingsley. "You have such a magnificent body, Miss Thompson," he said with a smile as his hands rubbed over her breasts.

Ashton gasped as she reached behind her and popped off her bra. "Ashton, professor," she reminded him with a smile.

"Of course," he said. "Forgive me."

"Forgiven, professor," Ashton chuckled.

She gasped in delight as she watched Professor Kingsley pull off her bra and proceed to squeeze her breasts. He licked his lips as he pulled her in and sucked gently on her erect knobs. Ashton felt his piece quiver against her thigh as he still seeped with pre-cum. She pushed her breasts into his face as it was clear he really enjoyed that. After several moments of nipple sucking and kissing around her areolas, Professor Kingsley wrapped his arms under her butt and around her thighs. He stood quickly, hoisting her up into the air.

Ashton did her best not to squeal. "Professor! You're an animal!" she gasped.

"Only with my most fondest of admirers," he joked as he laid her out on top of his mostly empty desk.

The heavy breathing on both ends intensified as the professor proceeded to kiss down Ashton's chest and stomach. He pulled up her skirt and proceeded to kiss further down between her legs. He could feel the warmth of Ashton's wetness as he slowly pulled off her panties. Ashton quivered in delight as she watched Professor Kingsley take in her clitoris with his mouth and sucked on it. She gasped in pleasure as she could feel his tongue dip inside between her pussy lips.

Professor Kingsley wanted Ashton to know he was no slouch, as he proceeded to rapidly thrust his tongue in and out of her. Ashton writhed with pleasure on the desk, completely caught off guard by this return of oral stimulation. Ashton did her best not to moan too loudly as she thrusted her body back up against his mouth.

Next, the professor pushed his finger inside her as he continued to suck on her clit. Ashton jumped as her whole body clenched in a pleasured reaction. The professor could feel her wet walls as they tightened on his finger as he proceeded to push as second one inside her. Ashton felt her whole body giving in to the immense amount of lust she felt for Professor Kingsley. She thrusted back against his body harder as she wanted to feel him push as deep inside of her as possible. "Oh god professor," she moaned quietly.

"I know I wanted to pass, but what I really want more than anything is for you to fuck me."

"That I can entertain with pleasure," said Professor Kingsley as he spread Ashton's legs wide open.

Ashton watched in anticipation as she grabbed her breasts and writhed in the overload of ecstasy. "I am on birth control, I don't want you to wear a condom," she whispered to him.

She watched as the professor stood and dropped his pants. Her eyes widened as she didn't fully realize just how well endowed he was through his pants. She gasped as she felt the full length of his shaft press between her lips and move up and down against her clit. He pushed his cock down as he situated himself against Ashton's thighs. He slowly pushed in with ease having been well lubricated with pre-cum and Ashton's juices.

"Oh my god you're so big," she moaned.

The professor smirked as he clasped his hands around her waist and proceeded to thrust vigorously into her. The desk was bolted to the floor, making it a sturdy piece to handle the rigorous movement of their back and forth motions. The professor grunted from how wonderfully tight Ashton felt as he went in as deep as he possibly could. He licked his thumb and used it to play with Ashton's clit just as something extra. Ashton's whole body shook in climax as she felt herself struggling not to scream with orgasm. She bit down on her lip hard as her body arched on his desk. The professor rolled his hands up under Ashton's back and held her gently as she rode out her orgasm against his cock.

In a second, he then flipped her onto her stomach, her bare breasts pressing down against the cool surface of his desk. He spread her legs open and pushed himself up inside her, the new angle making it tighter and far more pleasurable. He grunted as Ashton could feel him throbbing inside of her. She knew he was close and she was ready for him. Professor Kingsley continued to pump deep inside of her, letting the full length of his shaft caress her inner walls. She gasped as his head pushed against her cervix.

"I'm cumming," he warned her.

Ashton gasped and nodded happily as she pushed back against his cock. All at once she pushed him back and dropped to her knees. She grabbed his shaft with one hand and his balls with the other and pushed him deep into her mouth. She milked his cum as he ejaculated down her throat and let Ashton drink up every last drop. Ashton moaned on his member with pleasure as she couldn't explain how much she enjoyed the taste of his seed. He pulled out slowly as their eyes met, each of them grinning ear to ear.

" Well, Ashton," said Professor Kingsley as he stepped back and quickly pulled up his pants and tucked himself away. "I must say, you have provided me with a convincing argument to save your grade with a very generous and unscrupulous curve with your final exam."

"That sounds wonderful, professor," said Ashton as she followed suit in quickly getting dressed. "Perhaps after that, we could discuss how we will proceed with the Advanced Biology course you teach that I will have to take to fill in my credit hours."

"I'll be looking forward to those discussions," said Professor Kingsley with a smile. He sat back down, readjusting his tie as he finished fixing his shirt and suit. "Anything else I can do for you until then, Ashton?" Ashton finished fixing her blouse and hair as she grabbed up her books from the edge of the desk and smiled at him. "You can keep the panties, professor," she said with a seductive wink before grabbing the knob of the door and hurrying out before anyone could notice it was locked.

Professor Kingsley watched her go as he reached down and casually picked her panties up off the floor and snuck them into his pocket. He chuckled and sat back in disbelief in his chair. "With pleasure," he mumbled quietly to himself.

Birthday Billionaire Blowout

God, it's been a long day.

Meeting after meeting with unsuspecting board members; shy, mouse-grey interns scurrying up and down office corridors; a stack of paperwork in his inbox, ten inches high.

The height of a man's inbox should never rise to the length of his dick, thinks Aiden crookedly to himself and enjoys his own confident humor.

But he assumes that everything came with the territory. Just as he had passed his third decade, the company he had inherited from his father had overtaken its fiercest competitor in the marketplace, and so Aiden's bank account had finally passed the nine-figure mark. His "birthday billionaire blowout," as he liked to call it, had been an alcohol-soaked stain of breasts and booze, so much so that Aiden soon could no longer distinguish between the strippers and the women on the guest list, so desperately everyone threw themselves at him in their unrestrained stupor.

Yes, so the whole thing had certainly been worthwhile. He is still not sure who was the one who finally got him released, or how it had come about in the first place, but this night of debauchery had purified him.

Today, however, he longed for a different kind of cleansing, and if the hands of the clock are right, he had better hurry and prepare himself.

Aiden strolls down a modern hallway sprinkled with expensive artwork specially selected by his senior art consultant. He makes his way to his bedroom, the huge king bed, perfectly made and furnished with decorative pillows.

With deft fingers, Aiden unties the Windsor knot that holds his tie and throws his suit jacket on the floor, where it falls into a puddle of charcoal grey. Melinda will pick it up again later. The same nimble fingers work their way down his shirt and undo the buttons with a deft ease, revealing a dyed belly above a deep V of the pelvis.

This too, together with his trousers, makes the belt buckle clang. And finally the boxer shorts, constricting elastic waistband that was finally torn from his hips.

His cock hangs down and he tugs at it longingly, but there is no time until Marie comes and he hates being interrupted so much. He wouldn't want to take out his frustration on the young woman.

When the doorbell rings, a loud ringing sounds through the air, and Aidan hurries to put on his navy blue and silk bathrobe - he puts the belt around his waist and ties it into a knot as he walks back down the hall to the foyer where, through the private glass windows that frame the oak door, he can see that Marie is floating on his doorstep.

His cock is still half hard from those few long blows and the thought of pushing him into something warm and moist, but he has already made her wait.

So he opens the door wide, a glow of lust warms him as he catches the flash of her eyes down to his pelvis and then up again.

"Marie?" he asks.

"Yes, sir," she replies in a low voice, and Aidan suppresses a grin. She has good instincts. Or maybe the agency had sent a memo. Or maybe Collette had passed along the knowledge of his preferences after he let her go. Delays can't be allowed.

But Marie had what it takes to be a good substitute.

The V-neck of her dress, issued by the agency, drops just deep enough to expose the soft curve of her décolleté, whose soft material embraces her at every turn. She looks at him anxiously, but eagerly, and he immediately knows that she must be a new hire. The newcomers were always anxious to please him.

"Let me show you the terrace," he tells her, turns around and gestures inside. She steps forward and Aidan drops a hand on her back, lets it slide down a little too far and leads her into the house, her little satchel clinking with the oils on her side.

"We'll be working on a terrace?" she asks, obviously not used to the concept of doing her service outdoors.

"Oh, yes," replies Aiden with a slight upward twitch of his lips - more a suggestion of mischief than a smile. "But don't worry. It's pretty remote. I'm sure you'll enjoy it."

"I'll take your word for it," Marie replies, and something in her tone makes Aidan think there might be more to her than just a shy girl. Another side, maybe.

He leads her through the French doors to the terrace and holds his hand in this too low place, satisfied as they walk all the way to the massage table without her squirming or asking him to move it. But for Aidan, this was a practiced game. A natural ease to find out how far he could go.

Marie turns away as he undresses, but Aidan knows the effect he has on women. I'm sure she's curious, if nothing else.

The area is lush and green, trees and shrubs transform the backyard into what many women he had brought here had called the "fairy garden".

He lies down on the table, and a moment later Marie puts a blanket over his lower back and buttocks and begins to exercise his muscles, working her tiny but strong fingers into his knots and kneading them until his body bulges upwards in her touch and she has to guide him down again.

Her hands work so quickly and so skilfully, bringing deep physical pleasure that spins his head. In him the longing rises that her hands should move under the blanket she had draped over him at the beginning, and so something else also rises.

It is as if the pleasure and longing that encapsulates his muscles have nowhere else to go, his body has no other way to deal with it but to let blood rush down, let his cock get stiff and hard and long for redemption.

It takes every bit of Aiden's willpower not to grind into the bed beneath him just to get a little of the satisfaction his cock is calling for.

He moans as Marie digs deep into the curve of his shoulder blade and runs her fingers down, down, down.

"Does it feel... feels good?" asks Marie cautiously, but Aiden swears he can detect a hint of intrigue there, a double meaning of the question he knows Marie is probing to see if the rumours are true. If he asks her.

"That's my line," he blames her as if she were a misbehaving schoolgirl.

"Oh, oh", she mumbles and then giggles.

If there was any doubt at all whether she wanted him to ask her, he'd leave now. But at the time, Aidan expected it. They always wanted him to ask. Dirty whores, all of them. All it takes is the promise of a bunch of hundreds and a look at his perfectly toned body, and they become putty in his hand. He'd even made some of them beg for it, the feeling of his cock in their hands, making them wet and desperate. But Daddy doesn't reward begging. Daddy rewards achievement. Because in reality, the bundle of cash, as tempting as it may be, is not the reward, not the tip for a job well done. No, he had a very different way of showing his gratitude.

"But we are nearing the end of our time," Marie informs him.

Hm, how quickly an hour goes by.

"Of course," replies Aiden and slides himself under the blanket, turns on his back and leans on his elbows.

Now that he has turned around, his aching tail is hard

to miss, stretching the soft tissue and twitching with hope. Marie's eyes focus on it, the desire shimmers. She licks her lips as if she doesn't know she's doing it. For a long moment Aiden lets the uncertainty between them linger in the air, turning Marie's beautiful cheeks a deep pink, her soft, flaky lips slightly parted.

"So before we finish, I would like to ask for a full body massage," smiles Aiden.

"That's, uh, that's extra, sir," stammers Marie, clearly trying to make sure the two are on the same side before she makes a move.

"Oh, I know. It won't be a problem, I've arranged the payment. Now, shall I remove the sheet or will you be a good girl and remove it for me?

"I'll be a good girl, sir."

She steps around to stand by his side and Aidan looks up at her as she pinches the towel in each hand and slowly pulls it from his body, exposing his rock-hard cock, which rises hungrily six inches into the air. The towel falls to the ground with a soft blow, but Aiden doesn't hear it because he is too distracted by Marie.

"Oh", she gasps, her deep brown eyes widening at the sight of his cock. The sound she makes at the back of her throat is involuntary, random and oh so telling.

"You like what you see, don't you?"

Instead of answering, Marie makes another tiny moan.

"I bet the sight of my cock makes the pussy nice and wet, doesn't it? Better not let it distract you from your work."

"No, sir, of course not, sir. May I begin?"

"What a good girl, asking permission," purrs Aiden. "You may."

With that, Marie raises her hand and runs her sweet pink tongue across the palm of her hand, which is covered in saliva. Twice she does this with agonizing slowness until her palm is shiny and smooth.

"Let me relax you, sir," she pulls and wraps her long, slender fingers around his cock, lubricates the saliva, teases his head and makes sure his shaft is completely covered.

Aiden sighs briefly and marvels at how soft Marie's hands are as they move up and down his cock and tie him up with a twisting movement of the wrist as he lifts up.

She works slowly at first, strokes in a steady rhythm, making him sway in a comfortable suspension of lust, not so much that he has to fight not to come, but so much that he is desperate for her to continue.

A moment later, she adjusts her grip by holding his cock so that with each stroke her thumb hits the sensitive spot at the base of his cock head and with each touch triggers a slight jerk of his legs.

Marie's eyes are longing as she stares incessantly at his swollen cock, and Aidan snaps to attract her attention by temporarily shifting his focus from his own pleasure to hers.

"Come closer now."

She obeys and doesn't miss a beat as she strokes it.

"Use your other hand. Tuck up your skirt and pull your panties aside for Daddy. I want to see how wet you are."

After careful consideration, Marie lets one hand slide over her body, pauses to caress her tits and pulls up the hem of her dress to reveal a pointed black thong barely big enough to grab her bulging pussy lips.

"Pull her aside, Marie."

Marie follows his command, brushes her panties to the side and holds them there, giving Aiden full access to her pussy. As his hand gets closer, her hand wraps around his cock, making him shudder. He strokes along her slit with an index finger and enjoys the juices that collect there. He takes a moment to swirl the padding of his finger around her clitoris, already swollen with lust.

She emits a sharp moan.

"Quiet," Aidan demands and holds up his soaked index finger. "Cleanse him, whore."

Obediently, Marie tilts her head, bends down to wrap her tender, chubby lips around his finger, swirls her tongue around the tip as if it were the head of his cock, and Aidan's eyes close, a gasp escapes his lips.

He can imagine it so perfectly, her lips tight around his

cock, gliding up and down, up and down. Her tongue, licking at the tip, sucking and whirling, teasing him and forcing him closer to the edge.

Marie moans around his finger.

"I thought so," he smiles contentedly and shares her lips with his fingers before plunging one into her, her tight hole swallowing him. He rubs against her G-spot, firm movements in time with the jerk of her hand around his cock. He revels in the way her hole nestles around his fingers, warm and smooth and soaked in her juice. What a good, wet little girl.

Aiden removes his finger and pushes it sideways to the top of her slit where her clitoris is swollen and begging for his attention.

Her moans turn into almost lustful moans as he rubs himself in angry circles. He lets her enjoy it for a minute by letting her work ever closer to him before he moves on to a new technique.

Marie's clitoris is so dammed up in her desire for orgasm that Aiden can pinch it between his fingers, and he does. He rolls her between his thumb and forefinger, intensifying her screams and her pleasure. And just when she seems to be about to climax, he lets go of her completely.

"Unnf," she moans. "Please, please, sir... . . .oh, God. . . . . . .please give it to me. I need it. God, my clitoris is throbbing, please."

Your begging gives Aidan a wave of joy and a satisfied grin.

"You want me to keep going, bitch? You want to cum for me like the dirty whore that you are? I bet you're desperate for me to cum on you."

"Oh, ooh, I do, sir. Please, please, please finish me off, I need it so bad, I'm begging you. Finish me off."

Aidan just looks at her for a moment and judges the

waves of lust that roll down his aching cock and bring him closer and closer to the edge. A moment later, he made a decision.

"Finish it," he orders, and he realizes that she was itching for it, that she longs for it because the hand that wasn't busy stretching his dick is flying to her clitoris. He takes cruel pleasure in forcing the girl to settle for second best, and he knows that nothing will ever satisfy her as he could have, that the thought of his deft fingers working her clitoris will stick in her memory. That the memory will always rise again. Whether she is alone or with another man, she will allow the memory to push her over the edge.

And Marie seems to know it. Her hands work faster and faster, she increases in speed, just as her two moans increase in volume. God, he can feel his climax coming, rising, powerful and overwhelming.

He uses his freshly freed hand to push the collar of Marie's V-neck to the side, and works his hand inside her bra to pinch her hard, pointy nipples between his fingers, just as he had done a minute earlier with her clitoris.

Maybe this is what finally sends Marie over the edge, but Aiden feels her climax before she reaches it and tells her

"That's right. Be a good girl. Lock up for me, my little whore."

And she does it, her body twitching and shaking as she moans in ecstasy, eyes rolling back into her head.

Her hand tightens around his cock as her orgasm unmasks her and puts her back together again, and the effect of all this, her hand, the pressure, her moaning, her supple tits and the way she begged for him and the resulting desire to deny her makes him go over the edge.

From the tip of his cock, thick, white sperm spurts out, dripping down the side in hot, rope-like strands.

"Cleanse him."

"Yes, sir," Marie says, bowing her head and nodding.

Her voice is soft and breathless, the girl is obviously still staggering before her orgasm, but she still obeys, bends over to run her tongue over his cock, licks up every trace of sperm, and leaves his cock sparkling clean. She swallows every trace of his cum with an innocent grin, has pieces of it smeared over her lips before licking them clean too.

"That's a good boy," Aiden says to her and runs her hand over the top and along the back of her head. A moment later he stands up, a satisfied tingling sensation buzzing up and down his legs.

He goes to a small shelf on the house wall and takes out a bundle of hundred dollar bills, counts them out for Marie and loves how greedily she stares at the cash - almost as hungry as she had stared at his cock.

He pushes the money into her hand and pulls her towards him to squeeze her ass one last time.

She giggles and Aiden looks at her for another moment. Yeah, he thinks she shows promise, sure. As long as she's on time, she'll do fine.

"I love stories with a happy ending, don't you?" asks Aiden and begins to pull at his silk robe, tugging at its silk robe, and laces the belt again to hide the rooster Marie had been so desperately drooling for.

"I do," confirms Marie, her voice still breathless. "Did I play to your satisfaction, sir?"

Aidan smiles again. "You can tell the agency to book another appointment next week for the same time. and make it twice as long."

"Of course, Sir," Marie says to him, giving her voice a tone of innocence with big eyes and makes her way back through the French door and through the front door, so that Aiden is more than satisfied.

9 781953 732743